Mary-Kate and Ashley
Sweet 16

Win a
$500
shopping spree!
Details on page 131.

Mary-Kate and Ashley
Sweet 16

Forget Me Not

By Cameron Dokey

■HarperEntertainment
An Imprint of HarperCollins*Publishers*

A PARACHUTE PRESS BOOK

A PARACHUTE PRESS BOOK

Parachute Publishing, L.L.C.
156 Fifth Avenue, Suite 302
New York, NY 10010

Published by
HarperEntertainment
An Imprint of HarperCollins*Publishers*
10 East 53rd Street, New York, NY 10022-5299

ISBN 0-06-059614-7

First printing: January 2005

Printed in the United States of America

Visit HarperEntertainment on the World Wide Web at
www.harpercollins.com

10 9 8 7 6 5 4 3 2 1

chapter one

"What about 'Midnight Madness'?" my best friend, Brittany Bowen, proposed.

The five of us—Brittany, myself, my sister, Mary-Kate, and our friends Lauren Glazer and Melanie Han—were sitting at a table in the food court of our local mall. Together we made up the theme committee for our high school's annual Spring Fling dance.

Our mission: come up with a theme that would set the mood for the event. "Midnight Madness" was just the latest of about ten thousand themes we'd already proposed.

Proposed. Considered. Rejected.

"Wait, I know! Don't tell me," Melanie went on now. "Too late-night-sale-at-the-mall."

She gave a sigh and plopped her head down

into her hands, her fingers digging into her curly brown hair as if trying to recharge her brain cells.

"I just can't believe this is so hard! How many lame ideas do we have, exactly?"

Across the table from me Mary-Kate, who'd been writing all our suggestions down—right before crossing them off one by one—looked up with a serious expression on her face.

"I'm not so sure you want to know."

Beside Mary-Kate, Lauren took a sip of soda. "You guys," she said, her green eyes concerned, "the entire junior class is counting on us to come up with a totally great theme. We cannot afford to screw this up. If we do, we'll have to change schools or something."

"Gee, Lauren," Melanie said, arching her dark eyebrows. "Apply the pressure much?"

"I hate to say this," I said, "but Lauren's right. Last year's Fling was the best ever. It's a hard act to follow, but we've got to come up with something."

"We know, but let's face it." Mary-Kate spoke up. "We've been at this since three-thirty, and so far we've been inspired about the same number of times we've been struck by lightning."

"Which would be zero, in case anybody's counting," Brittany added glumly.

"Maybe we should try coming at it from a new direction," I suggested, determined not to let the meeting come to a complete halt. "Just brainstorm. Free associate."

The other girls looked at me. Clearly I would have to keep going.

"What are the qualities that make a Spring Fling special?"

"Romance," Melanie said at once.

"Exactly!" I pounced. "Don't stop, Melanie. Go on. You've been dying to talk about it all day anyhow."

"Okay, wait. I'm officially confused," Lauren declared, waving her arm.

Mary-Kate grinned as understanding dawned. "Anthony Martin. Melanie. Hot date. Last night."

"Oh, that!" Lauren exclaimed. Then she frowned. "Wait a minute. Wasn't it supposed to be this weekend?"

"It turned out Anthony couldn't make it then," Melanie explained with a small smile. "So he asked if we could switch it to last night."

"Okay, hold everything. Stop right there," Brittany said. "You're saying a guy actually asked to go out on a date *ahead* of schedule?"

"Yep," Melanie replied.

3

Brittany shook her head, as if she couldn't believe what she was hearing. "Where did you find him?" she asked. "On Mars?"

"History class," Melanie said with a laugh. "About halfway down the row of seats closest to the door."

"Well, did you have a great time?" Mary-Kate asked eagerly. "Inquiring minds want to know."

Melanie looked down at the table, her smile now mischievous. "No," she pronounced firmly. "I did *not* have a great time."

"What?" Lauren cried.

"*Great* doesn't even begin to cover it," Melanie continued. She looked back up. "I had an absolutely incredible, impossible-to-describe-because-they-haven't-invented-the-words-yet time."

"Oh, wow," Brittany said, her brown eyes widening. "So I guess that means it went well."

A burst of laughter swept the table.

"Don't just sit there smiling, Mel!" Mary-Kate exclaimed. "We need details. And I mean every single one. Don't leave anything out." Her pencil hovered above the Spring Fling list, as if to record Melanie's every word.

"Actually," Melanie said, her tone growing thoughtful, "there's not that much to tell. That's the funny thing about it. We didn't do anything all that special. We just took a walk and went for a soda. It's more the way he made me feel. . . ." Her voice trailed off.

"And that's what?" I asked.

I was curious, I had to admit. Having semi-recently been through a painful breakup with my longtime boyfriend, Aaron Moore, I was interested to hear how Melanie's date had gone. I was eager to hear about a beginning instead of an ending, for a change. Especially a beginning that sounded so promising.

"He treated me like I was . . . important," Melanie went on. "You know how some guys always seem to be thinking of something else when they're with you? Like, they're afraid to pay too much attention, because you'll try to introduce the *L* for *love* word too fast?"

"I hear that." Brittany nodded.

"Well, being with Anthony wasn't like that at all. He was totally relaxed, completely in the moment. I felt like the only girl on Earth. I know that sounds kind of . . ."

"Impossible," Brittany said.

"Fabulous," Mary-Kate countered.

"Romantic." Lauren sighed.

"All of the above," I voted.

"You're going to ask him to the dance, aren't you?" Mary-Kate inquired.

"Absolutely." Melanie nodded vigorously. "Just as soon as we come up with a theme so there's a dance to take him to. Which reminds me . . ." She tapped Mary-Kate's list with the tip of her pencil. "Back to business."

"Hold everything. I'm about to be brilliant," Mary-Kate announced, her eyes wide. "How about 'Isn't It Romantic?' for a theme? Each section of the gym could feature a different thing people associate with being *in love*."

"The refreshment area could be Paris," Lauren instantly suggested. "We could bring in little bistro tables, make people feel they're at a sidewalk café. Everybody thinks Paris is romantic, right?"

"This is great! This is totally great!" Melanie said excitedly. "I think this idea could really work, you guys! Let's start making a list of mini-themes for the different parts of the gym. What about when people first come in? That's the obvious place to start."

Taking over from Mary-Kate, Melanie grabbed the list, turned it over, and began to jot down notes as the ideas flew fast.

All of a sudden I saw Mary-Kate's eyes widen again. She looked at me, then cast a glance meaningfully over my shoulder. Melanie, Brittany, and I were sitting facing into the food court, but from her position Mary-Kate had a clear view of the mall. There was something behind me I ought to see but probably didn't want to.

Aaron, I thought. Determined to be casual, I slid a napkin off the table onto the floor, then bent to pick it up. As I straightened, I cast a quick look back.

It wasn't Aaron. It was Melanie's date from last night, Anthony Martin. And he wasn't alone. He had his arm around a girl wearing a cheerleader's uniform from Westwood High, our school's crosstown rival. He was gazing at her as if . . . *as if she's the only girl on Earth,* I thought.

Uh-oh.

Melanie was going to have her heart broken, no two ways about it. She and Anthony only went out once, but it was pretty obvious that Melanie had fallen for him. Hard.

"Ashley, tell me what you think of this," I heard Melanie say. "How about, when people first come in . . ."

I heard the scrape of her chair as she turned

7

toward me. *Don't do it! Don't turn around!* I wanted to cry. Too late. I knew the second she spotted Anthony. Her normally tan face went pale, and she sucked in a breath.

"Melanie," I heard a guy's voice say, from somewhere in the general vicinity of above my head. It came out kind of high-pitched and funny. "What are you doing here?"

"It's a mall, Anthony. What do you think I'm doing here?" Melanie answered coolly.

❀

"I just don't understand it," she wailed several moments later as she rested her head on Ashley's shoulder.

The painful encounter with Anthony and his Westwood girlfriend was over. Melanie had come through with flying colors. She hadn't made a big ugly scene. Say, for instance, one that involved scratching Anthony's eyes out. She'd stayed cool and polite.

From the expression on the other girl's face, I had a feeling Anthony was doing a lot of explaining right now. I hoped he bombed. Big-time.

"Why would he even ask me out if he was already seeing someone else?" Melanie asked now. "It doesn't make sense."

Ashley gave her shoulder a consoling pat. "There's no accounting for guys' behavior."

"You can say that again," I said.

"There's no accounting for guys' behavior."

Melanie gave a snort of reluctant laughter. "Stop trying to make me feel better," she said. "I want some time to wallow."

"Wallow away," Lauren said. "You're entitled."

Reaching across the table, I pulled the list of our Spring Fling ideas toward me.

"Alright, so maybe 'Isn't It Romantic?' is a little over the top," I remarked, crossing it out.

"Why can't guys come with an instruction manual or something?" Brittany inquired.

"I sure could use one," Ashley said at once.

Immediately the entire table snapped to attention. Even Melanie sat up straight.

"Is it Aaron?" she asked.

Ashley nodded. "I got a voice-mail message from him last night. He wants to talk. About, and I quote, 'something important.'"

"Uh-oh," Brittany muttered.

"That's pretty much what I thought," Ashley remarked.

"Do you think he wants to get back together?" Lauren asked. "I mean, face it, he was a total idiot to break up with you," she added loyally.

"I honestly don't know," Ashley said. "And even if he does, I'm not sure that's what I want."

"Personally," Brittany said firmly, "I think you should move on. There's that cute new guy in math, Michael Hennessey. He's been checking you out."

"He has been trying to catch my eye, hasn't he?" Ashley said, her own eyes beginning to twinkle.

Lauren gave a snort. "You could say that."

"He could be gazing soulfully at you," I put in, "or he could be staring into space, desperately trying to solve one of Mr. Cohen's impossible trigonometry problems."

There was a short silence while we all considered the possibilities.

"Or that." Brittany nodded.

First Melanie's lips twitched, then Lauren's. Then all five of us began to laugh. At precisely that moment my cell phone rang.

"Are we still in a meeting?" I blurted out as I pulled my shoulder bag onto my lap and prepared to dig for my phone.

Coming up with the right theme for Spring Fling was so important, we'd all made a deal: no phone calls during meetings.

"I've had it for today," Ashley admitted, as my phone continued to warble. "My brain is totally fried. How about if we sleep on things, then try again tomorrow?"

"Sounds good to me!" I said.

Lauren rolled her eyes. "You just want to take that call," she said. "It's probably some guy."

"Don't do it, Mary-Kate!" Melanie cried theatrically.

I was laughing as I flipped open the phone. "Hello?"

"Mary-Kate, it's Liam," said the voice at the other end of my cell phone. "Remember me?"

11

chapter two

"Liam," I repeated, as if I'd never heard the name before. "Liam. Liam. Wait a minute. It's starting to come back to me."

I scooted back from the table so my conversation wouldn't disturb the others. Ashley gave me an amused look, and I grinned back.

"Liam McCaffrey," the voice on the phone said. "You know, from *Girlz* magazine? Liam who owes his current career in journalism to you? Liam who owes you a really big favor but is hoping you'll do him one instead?"

"Oh, *that* Liam!" I exclaimed. "Sure. I remember you."

He laughed, relieved.

Liam and I had been interns together at *Girlz* magazine. At first I'd thought we might be competitors, but instead we ended up working as a team and becoming friends. When summer vacation rolled around, I could have worked there full time, but I decided that lifeguarding was calling to me just a little bit more loudly. After that Liam and I sort of went our separate ways.

"I saw the article you did for that college paper not long ago," he went on now. "Great job."

"Thanks," I said. "Though being a high school student at college for a few weeks definitely had its weird moments." The experience had been part of a school project. "How are things at *Girlz*?" I asked.

"Good," Liam replied. "But there is something I'd really like to talk to you about. Any chance we could meet up?"

"Sure," I said, surprised and pleased. "Just say when."

"How does *now* sound?"

"Desperate," I answered.

He laughed. "You got that right."

"Half a second," I said. I turned back toward the table. "You need the car, right?" I asked Ashley.

"I do." She nodded.

"I can drop you somewhere," Lauren offered.

"That would be great. Thanks," I said. I turned

my attention back to the cell phone. "Is Click Café all right?" I asked.

"Perfect," he said at once. "I'll meet you there."

"Okay," I said.

"Liam—he's that guy you used to work with at *Girlz* magazine, right?" Lauren asked as I ended the call and put away the cell phone.

"Right," I said. "I haven't heard from him in months, but now he calls out of the blue and wants to meet."

"That's interesting," she commented as we gathered up our stuff. "I wonder why."

"So, I suppose you're curious why I called," Liam said a short time later.

We were sitting at my favorite coffee bar, Click Café. Lauren and I had headed right over, but Liam still got there first. Whatever he wanted to talk about, it must be important.

"That would be *yes*," I said.

Liam gave a quick smile, the gesture lighting up his whole face. I felt a funny tingle run through my body. He really was incredibly cute. How could I have let him slip to the back of my mind?

"It's this assignment I'm working on," he explained. "It's a new online column called

Expertise. Relationship advice for girls from a guy's point of view. It was CK's brainstorm, but she passed it on to me. It's my first big assignment."

"That's so cool, Liam! Congratulations," I said.

"Don't go there yet," he warned. "I'm so on the verge of blowing it, I can't believe it. And if that happens . . ."

He didn't have to fill in the rest. I remembered CK Fein, *Girlz* magazine's tough managing editor. She was like a tornado with legs. She never expected anything less than the best from her staff. If Liam blew his first big assignment, it was a pretty safe bet it would also be his last.

"So what's the problem?" I asked.

Liam gave a sigh and rested his chin on one hand. "First of all, you have to swear not to tell anybody about this—not even your sister," he said. "If CK finds out I've talked with someone outside the *Girlz* staff . . ." Dramatically he drew a finger across his throat to demonstrate the results.

"Sworn to secrecy. Got it." I nodded.

"I'm completely blocked," Liam confessed. "The column is supposed to launch on the Web site in two days, and my brain is frozen solid. I can't even decide on a topic for the first column.

CK wants, and I quote, 'something fresh.'"

"Uh-oh. Talk about pressure," I said.

"No kidding," Liam answered glumly. "I've been racking my brain for days, but every idea I come up with just feels so . . ." His voice trailed off.

"So not fresh," I filled in, sympathizing as I remembered the Spring Fling theme meeting I'd just come from. "Lame. Old. Stale."

"You're making me feel so much better already," Liam said dryly.

"Maybe you're trying too hard," I suggested, thinking of the approach Ashley had come up with—the one that had gotten our creative energy flowing at last. *"Don't* think. Just brainstorm. Free associate."

"Okay," Liam said at once. "You go first."

"Thanks a lot!" I made a face at him across the table. He made one right back. I could feel that funny tingle go through my stomach for a second time.

"Girls," I said.

"Math test," Liam answered without missing a beat.

"What?" I cried.

"Math test," he said again, as if the reason for this should be obvious to anyone with even half a brain.

"As in, what does it feel like to figure girls out?"

"Sorry I asked," I said. "Your turn."

"Guys."

"Aspirin. Because—"

"They're such a headache," Liam finished up with a grin.

"Yep!" I said. "So what did we just prove?" I was really getting into this now, the germ of an idea sprouting in the back of my mind.

Liam scrunched up his face in concentration. "I'm really going to hate myself in a second."

"Why's that?" I asked with a laugh.

"Because I know the answer's going to be really simple . . . but I can't figure out what it is."

"We just proved that you don't need a 'fresh' topic," I said.

"We did? How?"

I opened my mouth to explain.

"Wait a minute. Don't tell me. I've got it!" Liam interrupted. "You mean because the first thing we came up with is that girls don't get guys."

"I think you mean guys don't get girls," I countered.

Liam laughed. "Guys find girls mysterious, and vice versa. It's the oldest conflict in the book, but it's still true."

17

"So why not use that as a launch topic?" I suggested.

"Oooka-ay," Liam said slowly. He took a sip of his coffee, thinking it over. "But if I don't have a fresh topic, I'd better have a fresh approach."

"Such as?"

He wadded up his napkin and tossed it onto the table. "I haven't got a clue."

"Clues! That's it!" I said.

"That's what?"

"Your fresh approach," I said. "Can't figure the guy out? Stop expecting him to think and act the way you do! Instead, look for *clues* that can tell you how he really feels."

"Wait a minute," Liam said. "What clues? I love this idea, don't get me wrong. I just don't know what you're talking about."

"I'm talking about that thing every girl wishes she had," I said. "An instruction manual. A set of guidelines to help figure out the mysteries of guy behavior."

Liam sat up a little straighter. "Girls think guys are a mystery?" he said. "Now *that* is different."

I pointed at Liam's pen and notebook. "Stop making smart remarks and start writing this down," I said.

chapter three

You're in trouble, Ashley. No two ways about it.

Not only that, but there was no way I could call for reinforcements. Mary-Kate, our friends, and I had all gone our separate ways after the committee meeting broke up. I'd stopped to run a quick errand for my mom on the way to the mall's parking lot.

That was when it had happened: I spotted Aaron coming out of Electro-Mart, a store that stocks video games, CDs, and DVDs. And then *he* spotted *me*. His face turned bright red, and he stopped cold. Before I could even think about running for cover, he made his move, coming straight toward me like a torpedo homing in on its intended target.

So naturally I did the most graceful thing I could think of: I froze like a deer in a set of oncoming headlights. For several beats of my frantically pounding heart, my body refused to move. In that moment of absolute panic, the way I felt about having a serious conversation with my former boyfriend was suddenly crystal clear.

I did not want to go there.

I also didn't want to go there in the middle of a shopping mall. Malls are great for all kinds of situations, but serious relationship discussions aren't among them. Not unless I was having them with Mary-Kate or my friends, of course.

My body was screaming something like: *Go! Run! Now!* I didn't care if Aaron thought I was the world's biggest chicken. All I cared about was not talking about the big serious thing he wanted to talk about.

Pivoting on one heel, I turned my back on Aaron and walked briskly through the nearest open door.

By the time I realized it was a beauty salon— the one place it was a pretty safe bet Aaron wouldn't follow me into—sirens began blaring. A stylist in a white coat rushed forward and seized me by the shoulders, just as a bunch of brightly colored balloons tumbled down from the ceiling.

"Congratulations!" she shouted over the sirens'

wail. "You're our one hundredth customer. You've just won a free makeover! Come in and sit down! Charice, the owner, will be right with you. She wants to do the session herself."

I cast a quick look over my shoulder. Somewhat to my surprise, Aaron was actually hovering near the door. *That's it,* I thought. I wasn't so sure a makeover was what I wanted, but I *was* sure talking to Aaron wasn't!

I turned back to the stylist and gave her a smile. "Excellent," I said. "Any chance I could get you to turn off those sirens?"

Too bad I didn't think of getting this makeover before *I spotted Aaron,* I thought as I gazed into the hand mirror Charice, the salon owner, presented me a couple of hours later. *He'd never have recognized me.*

I wasn't so sure I recognized myself. The makeover was as good as any disguise.

My face had so much stuff glopped on it, my pores were screaming for air. My eye makeup made me look sort of like those pictures you see of Cleopatra: thick, dark eyeliner and bright blue eye shadow.

But the makeover hadn't ended there. I'd also

received a manicure and pedicure. My toes and nails were now painted in what I could have sworn was the same sparkly polish I wore last Halloween, when I dressed up as Tinkerbell.

And, finally, there was my hair.

I still couldn't quite figure out how Charice had accomplished this part of my transformation, and I'd watched her do it myself. She had waved the blow dryer around a lot, and the end result looked as if certain sections of my head had been hit by a tornado, while others had been spared. The parts that had experienced the windstorm stood straight up, while the rest lay absolutely flat, as if playing dead.

"Big change from when you came in, huh?" Charice beamed as she took back the hand mirror.

"Absolutely," I said truthfully.

I slid out of the chair. My knees wobbled. But disastrous as it was, there was nothing about the makeover that a good hot shower couldn't cure. Now all I had to do was to get to my car without being seen by anyone. Aaron had long since given up and left. At least that was good news.

"Let me give you one of our cards," Charice went on as she escorted me to the door. She reached into the pocket of her white coat, extracted a business card, and pressed it into my hand. "Remember, Salon Experience is the place to create a whole new you. Tell your friends."

"My friends will definitely hear all about this," I promised, trying to keep the sarcasm out of my voice. "Thanks."

As I moved back out into the mall, I glanced hopefully at the shops between me and the parking lot. With luck I could make a quick purchase.

A large purchase. That way I'd have a bag to put over my head as I made my way to the car.

"I am absolutely serious!" Mary-Kate exclaimed the next day at morning break. "She looked so different, I almost didn't recognize her. It's a good thing Mom didn't see her first. I don't think she'd have let her into the house."

"Oh, come on," Lauren said, laughing. "No makeover could be *that* bad."

I pulled the card Charice had given me out of my wallet and slid it across the table toward her.

"Salon Experience," I said. "Experience it for yourself and find out."

"Oh, no," she said. "Your experience was free. There's no way I'm going to pay to be turned into a walking disaster area."

"What on Earth possessed you to go into the salon in the first place?" Brittany asked.

"I was avoiding Aaron," I confessed, wincing.

"Ashley Olsen fails to meet a challenge head-on?" Melanie teased. "That's a switch."

"Could we possibly avoid the word *head*?" I asked. "My hair still feels as if it's trying to go back to the way it was when I left the salon."

"Hardly surprising," Mary-Kate remarked. "I think it must have contained an entire tube of extra-strength styling gel."

"You're talking about that piece in back sticking straight up, aren't you?" Brittany asked. At the alarmed expression on my face, she held up her hands. "Kidding!" she said.

"I hate to be the one to crack the whip," Melanie said, "but we've only got five minutes of morning break left. This is supposed to be a meeting. Shouldn't we be talking about the dance?"

"You're absolutely right. We should," I said, happy to get back on track. "I'm embarrassed to say I don't have any new ideas, and I'll bet I can say the same for Mary-Kate. By the time I got home, all I wanted to do was soak my head. Literally. I didn't even think about the dance."

"Ashley's right," Mary-Kate acknowledged.

"You guys," Lauren said sternly. "Let's take another night to think. Lunchtime. Tomorrow. Our favorite table outside. Be there with ideas, or else. We have got to get our act together!"

"I couldn't agree more," I said.

❀

"That's fantastic, Liam!" I said. "I can't believe you're going to launch a whole day ahead of schedule!"

"Me neither!" Liam said, his voice full of excitement at the other end of my cell phone. "In fact, I keep pinching myself. But CK loved your guidelines idea so much, she decided she didn't want to waste a moment getting it up and running. *Expertise* should be on the *Girlz* Web site by the time we're finished with this phone call. I really have to hand it to you, Mary-Kate. Without your help . . ."

I felt a warm glow of pride. I'd helped create a hit! It didn't matter that a lot of the ideas about to appear on the Web site were mine and I wouldn't be getting credit for them. It had been great working with Liam again. In fact, we really clicked.

"You'd have figured something out," I said.

"Not something as great as what we came up with together," Liam said promptly. "We make a good team, don't you think?"

You bet I do! I thought. "Thanks," I said.

"I'd like to take you out to dinner to say thank you," he said. "I know it's incredibly late notice, but is there any chance you're free tonight? I actually got reservations at Le Château."

"You're kidding!" I blurted out.

Le Château was currently one of the hottest dinner spots in town. It was a fabulous French restaurant which was in an old house extensively remodeled to resemble a French manor house. Which explained the restaurant's name.

I *had* planned to spend the evening doing my homework, then working with Ashley on a theme for the dance. But no girl in her right mind turned down an opportunity to go to Le Château. Especially when it meant going with such a promising guy. I *couldn't* say no. More than that, I realized how much I didn't *want* to. I wanted to see Liam again. It was as simple as that.

My friends would understand.

"Thank you, Liam," I said. "I'd love to go."

❁

Whew, I thought as the final bell sounded. Somehow I'd made it through the day. Without a major hair incident *or* an encounter with Aaron. He'd kept his distance, even though I caught him

26

looking over at me a couple of times in the classes we shared.

Why am I stressing so much over a conversation? I wondered as I joined the steady stream of students tossing some books in lockers and retrieving others before heading home. Every time I even thought about talking with Aaron, my stomach got tied up in knots.

It's the mystery of the whole thing, I thought now as I let my feet carry me out of the building to cut across the playing field near the gym. Aaron had said he wanted to talk to me about something important. In person. Not over the phone. But over the phone had been good enough to break up with me.

Well, actually that had been done at my front door at the end of a date, but it was confirmed later over the phone.

So what could be more important than breaking up? Getting back together, maybe?

"Hey, Ashley. Wait up!" I heard a voice yell. Instantly, my stomach felt as if I'd swallowed a load of bricks. I turned in time to see Aaron sprinting across the lawn. Apparently he wasn't taking any chances on my getting away.

"Oh, hi, Aaron. It's you," I said, my voice coming out funny. Way too high and cheerful, sort of like a Saturday-morning cartoon character's. "Listen, I'd love to stay and talk, but there's someplace I'm supposed to be," I said.

"What?" Aaron asked as he skidded to a stop beside me, slightly out of breath.

"I can't talk now. I'm supposed to be someplace else," I said. *Anyplace else.*

An expression I couldn't quite read flashed across his face. "Look, Ashley—" he began.

Then I saw my out.

"There they are, right over there!" I cried, cutting him off. "See you later, Aaron!"

Before he could get another word in edgewise, I was sprinting away from Aaron and across the lawn toward the gym. A group of girls in sports attire was clustered around the door.

"Ashley!" Ms. Nelson, the P.E. coordinator, said in surprise as I dashed up. "This is great. I didn't expect to see you here."

"Oh, well, you know . . ." I said. *If only I did.*

"You're a little late, but that's okay," Ms. Nelson said. "Go ahead and get suited up, then join us out on the field, and we'll get started."

That was the moment I noticed the piece of equipment she held in her hand. . . .

chapter four

"Field hockey!" I exclaimed. "You went out for an all-city field hockey team?"

"I didn't mean to!" Ashley wailed. "By the time I realized what was going on, it was too late to back out."

As I watched, she hobbled to her bed and flopped backward onto it, limbs outstretched. "I think every single muscle in my body is sore," she moaned. "Remind me never to go near a sports field again."

"I still don't understand how you got involved in the first place," I said, shaking my head.

Ashley gave a groan—whether of pain or embarrassment, I couldn't quite tell. "Two guesses," she said.

"Aaron and Aaron."

"Right on both counts." Ashley scooted backward to sit propped up against her headboard. "I have got to get a handle on this situation, Mary-Kate," she announced. "This makes two days in a row now that I've completely panicked when I saw Aaron. Both times with disastrous results."

I took a deep breath. I was all dressed and ready to go out for my dinner with Liam. Ashley hadn't even noticed, she was so stressed. Much as I wanted to keep my date, there are some things that just plain come first. Such as supporting your sister in her time of need.

"Do you want me to stay home?"

"You're going somewhere?" Ashley asked. She sat up even straighter as she took in my appearance. "Wait a minute. You're all dressed up in the middle of the week. What gives?"

"It's Liam," I said. I moved to sit on the end of Ashley's bed. Much as I wanted to tell Ashley the whole story, I knew I couldn't. Not yet, at least. I wanted to understand it for myself first. Besides, the new *Girlz* Web site was so popular at school, if word got out that I was working on it, sooner or later someone would post something to that effect on the site, and then Liam's job would be in jeopardy.

"He just got this big promotion at *Girlz*," I explained, sticking to the safe stuff, "and he wants to take me out to celebrate. He got reservations at Le Château."

Ashley's eyes widened. "You're *kidding* me," she said.

I shook my head.

"Wow. I'm impressed. Let me see if I'm getting this straight. He calls you for the first time in months just yesterday, and today he's taking you to Le Château?"

"That's pretty much it," I said, trying with limited success to hold back an excited grin. "But I'll stay home if you need to talk."

Ashley slid over to give me a hug. "That's so nice. I really appreciate it," she said. "I might be desperate, but I'm not insane. There's no way I'd ask you to give up your date at Le Château."

"You sure?" I asked.

"Absolutely." Ashley nodded. "In fact, it might even be good for me to spend the evening without sisterly backup. I need to figure out why I've suddenly turned into a walking disaster area around Aaron. I think that's something I should do on my own. But I want to hear all about your evening the minute you get home."

"You got it," I said. I stood and headed for the door.

"Though there is one thing you can do, now that I think about it," Ashley called after me.

"What's that?" I inquired.

"Order the fanciest chocolate dessert on the menu."

"Oh, do I *have* to?" I asked sarcastically. As I walked out, Ashley's laughter followed me down the hall.

❀

Alright, Ashley Olsen. It's time to get organized!

After Mary-Kate's departure I'd been kind of restless. No matter what I did, I couldn't seem to settle down. My mind refused to concentrate on potential themes for the Spring Fling. And for once homework was minimal and didn't take long. Finally, before my mood could disintegrate into a full-fledged mope, I remembered that the reason for Mary-Kate's big night out with Liam was that he'd just gotten a promotion at *Girlz*.

So I logged onto the magazine's Web site and there it was.

Expertise—Advice for girls from a guy's perspective.

I definitely had to check this out.

Is it a match made in heaven, or just another date with a space alien? Five ways to tell if he's the real thing, the header read.

Could this be more perfect? I thought.

Quickly I skimmed the column. The more I read, the more excited I got. Now I realized what had been wrong with my recent approach to the whole Aaron situation. All I'd been doing was letting my fears get the best of me. I didn't have my own plan of attack at all.

Time to put a stop to that! I thought. And the guidelines provided by *Expertise* looked like just the way to do it.

Okay, Aaron, you can have your conversation about "something important," I thought. *But not until I've figured out a few things first!*

Feeling better than I had in days, I downloaded the *Expertise* guidelines, printed them out, and got out my favorite pen. Then I grabbed a fresh notepad and titled the page: *Operation Aaron.*

This is going to work! I thought.

❀

"To Mary-Kate Olsen," Liam said as he raised his glass of sparkling water. "The best secret weapon a terrified writer ever had. Not to mention the best friend any guy could ask for."

We clinked glasses. The ice cubes in them tinkled cheerfully.

This is pretty much perfect, I thought. The only thing that could possibly make the evening better would be slightly less use of the word *friend* on Liam's part. Followed by a good-night kiss and a request for another date.

Whoa, girl. Slow down, I thought. This was supposed to be a thank-you dinner. As far as I could tell, I was the only one who'd figured out that Liam and I could be much more than friends. If I moved too quickly, I might scare him off.

"It's no problem," I said as I set my glass down on the snowy-white tablecloth. "Any time panic hits, dial my number." I gave Liam an encouraging smile. "Though, if that's the only time you call . . ."

"Of course not," he replied at once. "As a matter of fact, I—"

"Ahem." A quiet cough above our heads gently cut him off.

I looked up to see our waiter, who had glided up beside our table so silently, I hadn't even noticed. Service at Le Château was like that. It's one of the things that made the restaurant so romantic. Food and drink appeared precisely when you wanted them, almost as if by magic. But the waiters never seemed to hover.

Maybe they all have ESP! I thought.

"Might I interest the young lady and gentleman in some dessert?" he murmured, gesturing to an elaborate silver dessert cart.

"You might. Most definitely," Liam answered enthusiastically.

The waiter gave a glimmer of a smile. In the same understated way he'd accomplished everything else, he described the contents of the dessert cart.

"After you, Mary-Kate," Liam said when the waiter was done.

"I promised my sister I'd have the most decadent chocolate dessert available," I confessed. "Do you have a recommendation?"

"*Mais oui, bien sûr.* Yes, of course," the waiter replied immediately. He gestured toward the cart. "There are more elaborate desserts, it is true, but for the pure *chocolat* experience, there is no substitute for the chocolate mousse."

"Perfect!" I said. This time the waiter gave an actual smile.

"And for *monsieur*?" he inquired, turning to Liam, who ordered an apple tart with caramel sauce. The waiter glided off, pushing the cart in front of him, promising to return in a few moments with our desserts and decaf coffee.

Now's my chance, I thought.

All evening I'd been trying to figure out a way to bring Liam's and my relationship into the conversation. We'd talked about other things during dinner—mostly what we'd each been doing since our days together at *Girlz*. Just sort of catching up.

We were pretty much up to date now, though. It was the perfect time to introduce the topic of what the future might hold for us. And the more time I spent in Liam's company, the more sure I became. When it came to my future, I wanted him in it. This was a guy I could seriously fall for.

"Mary-Kate," Liam suddenly said, "we make a good team, don't you think?"

"Absolutely," I answered, somewhat surprised.

I could feel a tingle of anticipation start in the pit of my stomach. I'd been looking for an opening all evening, and now Liam had just provided me with the perfect one! Could it be that he felt the same way I did, and I'd somehow failed to read the signals?

"I'm glad to hear you say that," he went on. "I

know I've said thank you for helping me out, but . . ." He paused, seemingly at a loss for words. "This is going to sound incredibly stupid," he finally admitted. "But I'm going to say it anyhow.

"I don't just want to say thanks for helping me out of a jam. I want to say thank you for being my friend, Mary-Kate," Liam went on. "When I got totally desperate, you were the first person I thought of. Not only because I knew you could help, but because I knew I could trust you not to get the wrong idea about why I was calling."

The wrong idea?

Liam looked a little unsure of himself, so I had to fill in the blanks.

"You mean . . . I wouldn't automatically jump to the conclusion you were calling me after all this time because . . . you'd suddenly decided you couldn't live without me," I said slowly. Somehow I managed to keep my tone light in spite of the fact that the tingle in my stomach had suddenly turned into an ache.

"That's it exactly." Liam nodded, clearly happy he didn't have to spell it out. "Not that any guy in his right mind *wouldn't* be interested in you, of course," he added quickly, as if he'd just realized he might have insulted me.

"Which makes you what?" I asked with a smile. "Nuts?"

He made a face. "Probably."

Okay, keep it together here, Mary-Kate, I thought. If I let Liam see that his words had upset me, I could ruin the whole evening. Not to mention blowing my chances for the future. I'd managed to keep things light so far. It was important for me to keep it that way.

Fortunately for me, the waiter returned with our coffees and desserts at precisely that moment.

"So, where were we?" Liam asked when we were alone once more.

I made a split-second decision: focus on the positive. "You were saying what a great team we make," I prompted.

"That's right." He nodded. "What I'm trying to get at is, would you consider keeping our partnership going? I'd like you to be a part of *Expertise*, at least for the first couple of columns. You'd still have to work behind the scenes, though.

"Actually, what am I thinking?" he went on as if he'd just realized what he was proposing. "Why would you want to do a thing like that? There's nothing in it for you."

That's what you think, I thought.

"I'd love to keep our partnership going, Liam," I said with a smile. Instantly his face lit up, and I felt my stomach finally settle down. I was taking the right approach. "Do you have the next topic all picked out, or do we need to do another round of brainstorming?"

"It's all picked out," Liam said enthusiastically as he dug into his apple tart.

I tasted my chocolate mousse. It was absolutely to die for. *At least something is going right,* I thought sadly. Ashley would be both incredibly pleased and insanely jealous! Maybe they gave dessert doggie bags.

"Since the first column was about a topic near and dear to girls' hearts, CK and I decided column number two should go for something near and dear to the heart of every guy. We're calling it *How to Get Past the First Date*. That way, girls can sort of have the chance to see what guys go through."

I had to admit it was cute. "Sounds perfect," I said at once. Not only that, it seemed safe to assume some actual dating might be involved. That had definite possibilities, as far as I was concerned.

"How are you going to collect your data?" I inquired.

behave a little oddly, I wasn't about to tell him.

"Have you talked to her this morning?" Aaron persisted. "I saw her at Click, and she seemed really depressed. I just want to make sure she's okay, that's all."

"She's fine," I said. But I could feel a little spurt of concern snake its way down my spine. *Could* Ashley be depressed? She was sleeping when I got home last night, and I hadn't actually seen her this morning. I'd overslept after my date with Liam. Ashley was already gone by the time I'd finally crawled out of bed. I hadn't even been able to tell her about the leftover chocolate mousse waiting for her in the fridge.

Had something happened last night that I didn't know about? Had Ashley really needed me, and I wasn't there for her?

Stop, Mary-Kate, I commanded myself. Ashley had encouraged me to go out with Liam. If something really big and bad had happened while I was gone, finding out would be easy enough. All I had to do was ask her.

"I'm sure everything's okay," I said to Aaron. "But I'll make an extra effort to double-check."

"Okay," he said. "Thanks." He hesitated a moment, as if wanting to say more. "Mary-Kate, I . . ."

"That's where I'm hoping you'll come in," Liam answered. He took a quick sip of coffee.

Yes! I thought. Unfortunately, his next words dashed all my hopes.

"A series of test dates is already being set up," he went on. "I'm the guinea pig." He made a quick face. "But I'd like you to be nearby, taking notes. After each date is over, we can compare impressions of what went right or wrong. At the end, we'll come up with a series of pointers for the column."

Nearby? I thought. I'd have to observe Liam on a date with other girls?

"The cool thing is that the pointers will actually be something both guys and girls can use," he went on excitedly. "What do you think?"

I think I don't want to see if you really hit it off with one of them, I thought sadly. *But then again, maybe I'll learn something about Liam that I can use to see if there's anything between us.*

"Just let me know where and when and I'll be there," I promised.

Okay, so it wasn't precisely what I'd hoped for. Still, as Liam had pointed out himself, we *were* a good team. The longer I stayed involved in *Expertise*, the more time Liam and I would spend together. The way I had it figured, time was on my side. Sooner or later I was sure I'd find a way to make Liam realize there could be more to our relationship than just being friends.

After all, I thought as I attacked the last of the chocolate mousse, leaving a smidgen to take home for Ashley, *it's a girl's right to try to change a guy's mind!*

chapter five

"Ashley, remind me why I'm doing this again?" Brittany asked with a barely stifled yawn.

We were riding in her car early the next morning. Too early, as far as Brittany was concerned. She was lots of things, but a morning person wasn't one of them.

"You're doing this because you're my best friend," I reminded her as we pulled into the Click Café parking lot. "Because you'd do anything for me, including lending me moral support at any hour of the day or night."

"And coffee beverages will be involved, right?" Brittany asked. "Preferably more than one?"

"Absolutely," I replied.

"Okay," she said. "Then I'm in, as long as you're buying, of course."

"Operation Aaron, here we come," I said. I took a deep breath and opened the passenger door.

I'd spent most of the previous evening coming up with Operation Aaron, basing it on the *Expertise* guidelines. I have to admit, I'd been pretty impressed by them. The guidelines went right to the heart of lots of things about girl-guy relationships that girls find hard to deal with.

Like, say, for instance, how come guys act so much like guys all the time?

Best of all, from my standpoint, it went on to suggest clues to look for when it came to guy behavior. Situations you could set up to figure out what was really on his mind. As I'd read through the pointers, I formed my plan.

Aaron wanted to talk to me about something serious? Fine. But before I'd let him have his big conversation, he'd have to experience a few of mine. In short, I was going to give Aaron a relationship pop quiz. If he passed, maybe I'd consider getting back together if that's what he was after. We *had* had fun together during the time we'd been a couple, after all. But if Aaron failed . . .

Either way I'd put a stop to panic mode and use an organized approach. Not only was this definitely more like me, but it would also avoid further humiliating experiences—or so I hoped! Best of all, by the time I finally gave Aaron the opportunity to have the serious conversation *he* wanted, I'd know what *I* wanted, thanks to the *Expertise* guidelines.

This morning's expedition to Café Click was Operation Aaron, Phase One. As Brittany and I made our way across the parking lot, I cast one final quick glance at the first of the *Expertise* guidelines.

The rule books all say not to try to change him. Fine. But think about this: How much time have you spent trying to make yourself over to please a guy? If he can't love you for who you really are, chances are good he can't love you at all. So ask yourself the following question: Does he accept me for who I am, right now? If the answer's no, chances are he's not the one, and you're absolutely right to think he's Mr. Wrong.

I thought about that. *Who I am right now?* That would be a high school junior who was awake at what most certainly felt like the crack of dawn. And who was about to appear in public and at school in her grubbiest helping-Mom-around-the-house work clothes, including no makeup.

"You're sure about this?" Brittany asked as we approached Click Café's front door. She eyed my holey denims doubtfully. "I hate to sound like a total idiot, but I'm still not quite sure what you're hoping to accomplish with all this."

"To find out if Aaron accepts me—all of me," I said. "Not just the Ashley he thinks he knows."

"You're sure you don't mean Evan?" Brittany asked.

Evan had been my one and only dating experience following my breakup with Aaron, and he definitely hadn't accepted me for who I really was. When he'd discovered I wasn't the college student he thought I was, he'd pretty much dumped me on the spot.

"Maybe," I acknowledged. "What happened with Evan hurt—I admit that. But the point is still the same. If Aaron does want to be with me, he needs to accept all of me, all the time. That's why I'm dressed this way." I'd always taken real care with my appearance when we went out. Everyone knew I was a stickler for making a good impression, for appearing organized and together.

"Okay," Brittany said. "If you say so. Personally, I think you're either incredibly brave or absolutely insane. I haven't figured out which one it is yet, but as soon as I do, I'll let you know."

With that, she opened the door and gestured for me to proceed inside.

Click Café was filled with its usual morning crowd. Lots of young professionals getting drinks to go. A few mothers pushing toddlers in high-tech running strollers. And a core group of high school customers. When Aaron and I were a steady item, we'd often met at Click Café before heading to campus. He was a regular, which was why I'd figured finding him here would be a pretty safe bet this morning.

"There he is," Brittany whispered. "At that table in the corner."

"I see him." I nodded. *That's* our *table*, I thought with a sudden pang. When we'd been together, we sat there almost every morning.

"I'll go order while you go talk to him," Brittany whispered once more.

"You don't have to whisper," I whispered back. "Having him notice me is pretty much the whole point."

"Oh, right," she said in a normal tone of voice. "Not awake yet. Sorry." She took off for the ordering line.

Pulling in a steadying breath, I made my way

toward Aaron's table. He was concentrating on an open notebook, a slight frown between his eyebrows.

"Hello, Aaron," I said.

His head jerked up. "Ashley!" he said, obviously surprised.

I saw his gaze range quickly over me, then past me, as if he was checking out who might be coming in the door. *Is he expecting someone?* I wondered. But in the next moment that thought was all but forgotten as Aaron brought his attention back to me.

"Ash," he said, his frown deepening. "Don't take this the wrong way or anything, but are you alright? You've been acting pretty funny lately, and now you look . . ."

His voice trailed off, as if he were searching for the right word. "Depressed," he finally announced.

Great. Just great, I thought. Sure I might look a little pale without my usual makeup, but depressed? I didn't think so.

"I'm fine," I answered curtly. "Besides, what would I have to be depressed about?" *It wouldn't be something like my longtime boyfriend's breaking up with me, now, would it?*

Aaron's face turned a dull red, almost as if he

47

heard what I was thinking. "That did not come out the way I meant it to," he said. "Sorry."

"That's okay," I said. "So, I guess I'll see you around."

"Ashley, wait!" Aaron said as I moved away from the table.

I stopped and turned around. At precisely that moment the door of Click Café opened. A group of our fellow students crowded in. "That's okay," Aaron said. "Never mind."

"Hey, Ash," I heard Brittany call. "Our drinks are up."

"Coming," I called. Suddenly determined to put as much distance as possible between me and Aaron, I spun around and headed for the counter.

"So," Brittany asked quietly as we collected our drinks, "how'd it go?"

"He asked me if I was depressed," I said.

Brittany gave a wince that I was pretty sure had nothing to do with the temperature of her beverage. "Ouch. So, I guess that means . . . you know."

"It certainly does."

If asking a girl if she was depressed equalled accepting her for who she was, I'd eat my latte cup. Aaron had just blown the first guideline. Big-time.

"Let's get out of here," I said.

"Whatever you say," Brittany seconded supportively.

Together we made our way to the door. I was just turning the handle when the door opened from the outside. Caught off balance, I lurched forward, barely avoiding spilling my latte.

"Sorry," a guy's voice said at once. "I didn't see you."

"That's okay," I said, letting my forward momentum carry me out the door without looking back. "Happens all the time."

Like a homing pigeon, I headed for Brittany's car. It wasn't until we were halfway to school that I realized what had happened.

"Please tell me that wasn't who I think it was."

"Depends on who you think it was," Brittany replied. She slid a glance in my direction, as if gauging my mood. "Do you want me to give you the easy out, or do you want the best-friend-tough-love stuff?"

"It was Michael, wasn't it?" I asked. "Cute Michael from math class, and I totally blew him off."

"I wouldn't say you blew him off," Brittany said as she negotiated a corner and pulled into the school parking lot. "It was more like you steam-rolled right over him."

I gave a groan. How much worse could my morning get?

"So," Brittany said as we climbed out of the car. "You're ready for that history test, right?"

"Mary-Kate, can I talk to you for a second?" a voice behind me said.

I shut my locker with a *clang*, then turned in surprise. My ears hadn't been playing tricks on me after all. I thought I'd recognized that voice.

"Hello, Aaron," I said. "What's up?" My tone wasn't all that welcoming. I didn't want to give him the silent treatment, but I didn't exactly want to casually chat with him, either. Ashley hadn't asked me to take sides; she wouldn't do that. But I knew that Aaron had hurt her a lot.

"Look," he said quickly, as if he knew what I was thinking. "I know you might not want to see me right now, but I need to know what's going on with Ashley. She's been acting really strange."

"Nothing's going on," I said.

Aside from the general freak-out she was having about the "serious conversation" Aaron wanted. If he couldn't figure out why that might make Ashley

50

At that moment the warning bell for first period rang.

"Omigosh!" I suddenly exclaimed. "First period. History test. I've got to go, Aaron. Catch you later."

I turned and sprinted down the hall toward my first-period classroom. It might be too late to cram for the test, but, with luck I could get there in enough time to check in with Ashley.

What was going on?

chapter six

Thank goodness that's over! I thought a couple hours later as I entered the cafeteria for morning break. First a test in history, followed by a pop quiz in science. Then, no sooner had the bell rung for morning break than my counselor, Ms. Latz, had caught me in the hall. I needed to make an appointment with her to talk about colleges, she reminded me. By the time we finished that conversation, break was half over.

How much more challenging could one morning get?

Not only that, I still hadn't had a chance to corner Ashley. I spotted our friends across the cafeteria, sitting at our usual table, deep in conversation. Instantly I headed toward them. But when I was halfway across the cafeteria, my cell phone trilled. Quickly I dug it out of my bag. An ID check showed the caller was Liam.

I have to take this, I thought. Not only had I promised him my continued help with *Expertise,* but the more I'd thought about it, the more I realized I didn't particularly want Liam going out on his test dates without me!

"Liam, hi! Hang on a minute," I said as I changed direction, heading for the nearest exit. I caught Lauren's wave out of the corner of my eye. I waved back but kept on going. The cafeteria was way too crowded to take a call. Not only would I have a hard time hearing Liam, but I might also accidentally give away my connection with *Expertise.*

"Sorry about that," I said once I was safely outside. I made for a spot under a nearby tree. "I was in the cafeteria and couldn't hear myself think. What's up?"

"The first date's all set," Liam's voice announced in my ear. "Can you make it today at lunchtime?"

"Just tell me where," I said, trying to ignore the way my spirits threatened to plunge. Knowing I didn't want the dates to happen without me and actually looking forward to them were two different things.

"The hot dog stand on the beach," Liam answered. "Twelve-fifteen, sound okay?"

"Absolutely," I said. Fortunately for both Liam and me, our schools had pretty cool off-campus policies. Both juniors and seniors were allowed to leave school for lunch. On lots of campuses only seniors had that privilege.

"See you then," I promised.

"Thanks," Liam said. We rang off.

When I was halfway back to the cafeteria, the bell rang. Morning break was over. I still hadn't talked to Ashley, and now lunchtime was out. At the rate I was going, we'd be seniors by the time I finally figured things out!

❀

"Hey, Ashley! Catch!"

Acting on instinct, I turned toward the voice. I was just in time to see a bright red apple shoot up into the air and sail over the tables in the crowded lunchroom, on a collision course with my nose. Right before it could make contact, I whipped out my hand and caught the apple in midair.

"He shoots! He scores!" came a shout from the guys at the table where the apple had originated. I recognized a group of sophomores who were always trying to make an impression on upperclassmen girls. Usually, though, they came off as childish and annoying. Their current lunch stunt only proved my point. A girl ought to be able to get from one side of the cafeteria to the other without fear of food hitting her in the face.

"You guys seriously need to get a life," I advised as I tossed the apple back in their general direction.

I was on the lookout for Mary-Kate. I'd been trying to connect with her all morning. I thought I'd caught a glimpse of her at morning break, but she'd ducked out, so I'd been forced to wait till lunch. Naturally, I wanted to hear how her evening with Liam had gone. But I also wanted to tell her about Operation Aaron. Not that there was particularly good news on that front; he'd flunked the first guideline.

Don't jump to conclusions, Ashley, I counseled myself as I continued across the cafeteria, ignoring the general lunchtime chaos and staying focused on my own thoughts. If I jumped to a conclusion too early in the game, I'd only set up a situation where what I *expected* to happen *would* happen. I was pretty sure there was even a name for that; I just couldn't quite remember what it was.

Yes, Aaron had bombed out on guideline #1, but there were still four more to go. Each one would bring me closer to knowing how I felt about the possibility of our getting back together. All I had to do was keep calm and . . .

"Hey, Ash," I heard a voice say.

I stopped. Without realizing it, I'd walked from one side of the lunchroom to the other. Straight to the table where Aaron and I always used to sit with our friends. A place I'd pretty much avoided ever since our breakup. Now it appeared that my legs had carried me there on autopilot while my brain was occupied with other matters. *Thanks a lot, legs,* I thought.

"Hi, Aaron," I said. I let my eyes roam across the sea of faces at the table. Maybe it was from the shock of finding myself in the last place I wanted to be in, but the faces all seemed blurry and out of focus. Aside from Aaron's only one stood out: that of the girl sitting directly across from him. *That's Suzanne, the new girl,* I thought. She was looking at me with big dark eyes, as if I were a wild animal who might do something unexpected at any moment.

Great. Somebody else who thinks I look dangerously depressed, I thought.

"So," I said. "How is everybody?"

There was a mumbled chorus of "okay"s and

57

"fine"s. Aaron stayed silent, staring down at his plate as if hoping the daily special would provide him with inspiration for something to say.

Not very likely. If memory served, the special today was meat loaf.

"Well, guess I'll see you all around," I said. I began to move off. The fact that I'd sounded completely lame was second only to how lame I must look, I thought, walking back the way I'd come, as if I'd purposely crossed the room for no better reason than to totally humiliate myself.

At least I made an effort to seem normal, I thought. Which was more than I could say for Aaron. He could hardly bring himself to look at me, let alone make conversation.

Omigosh, I thought. Without warning, I stopped short.

"Hey," an irritated voice at my back said. "What gives? Watch where you're going."

"Sorry," I mumbled as whoever I'd annoyed brushed past me. Not that I was paying all that much attention to what was going on around me. My hands were already opening my shoulder bag, searching for the *Expertise* guidelines.

Unless I was very much mistaken, Aaron had just flunked his second guideline of the day.

❁

How to Get Past the First Date, I wrote, then paused, pen poised.

I was sitting on a bench not far from the hot dog cart at the beach Liam had chosen as the location for his first "date." In honor of my new role as an undercover advisor, I'd unearthed a floppy sun hat from the trunk of the car, put on my biggest, darkest pair of sunglasses, and turned to a fresh page in my new notebook. Now that I was here and in place, I had to admit that my spirits were starting to pick up.

During dinner at Le Château Liam had explained that the magazine had run a telephone contest to select girls willing to take part in the research phase of future articles. The girls Liam would be "dating" were among those chosen.

He was already in place, hanging out by the hot dog cart. My bench location was the perfect observation spot. Close enough for me to see and hear but not so close that I'd be noticeable— unless I did something to draw attention to myself. With my notebook in my lap, I was hoping I looked like any other high school student catching a few rays while studying on lunch break.

"You're Liam, right?"

The sound of a girl's voice snapped me to attention.

"You must be Julie," Liam said with a smile. The two shook hands. Liam's first "date" was slim and tall. She had long dark hair pulled back in a ponytail. Her clothing was on the informal, athletic side. She looked as if she was about to go for a run.

"It's a pleasure to meet you. Thanks for coming," Liam went on.

"You're kidding, right?" Julie said with a laugh. "*Girlz* is my favorite magazine. I couldn't believe it when they called. I thought one of my friends was playing a joke or something."

"No way." Liam smiled. He gestured toward the hot dog cart. "What do you say we grab a bite, then talk?"

A strange expression flitted across Julie's face. "You actually want me to *eat* a hot dog?" she blurted out. Then she held up a hand. "Okay, wait. That *so* did not come out right. What I'm trying to say is . . . I'm a vegetarian!"

"That went well," I said. "For about the first minute or so. After that—"

"Okay, okay." Liam cut me off. "You don't have to rub it in. I know. It was such an obvious thing to ask, and it never even occurred to me."

"On the plus side," I continued with a smile, "it did give me a cool idea for pointer number one."

"Let's hear it," Liam said. He leaned back on the bench and closed his eyes.

I cleared my throat and read: "'How to Get Past the First Date, Pointer Number One: Don't wait until the date itself to ask yourself, or her, the following question: Are you planning to do something you can both enjoy? A moonlight cruise might sound romantic, but not if your date gets seasick at the sight of water. Save the surprises for after you've gotten to know each other. In the beginning check out your plans ahead of time.'"

Liam was silent for a moment. "You make it sound so simple," he remarked at last, opening his eyes. "That's a great first pointer. Even if you did come up with it at my expense. Guess I'd better double-check to make sure date number two's okay with meeting at the mall."

"That might be the exception that proves the rule," I said with a laugh. "I never met a girl yet who'd turn down a trip to the mall."

"Just so long as you're there to back me up," Liam said.

"Sure." I nodded, wishing we were discussing

our own plans instead of Liam's with a total stranger. *Be patient, Mary-Kate,* I thought. "Just let me know the day and time."

"Actually, it's today, after school," Liam said. "The dates are as back to back as we could make them, so they'd all be today. It's the only way I can make the deadline. Didn't I mention that before?"

"Nope," I said with an inward wince. "But don't worry. It's fine." Today after school was the next scheduled meeting of the Spring Fling theme committee. To cut down on distractions and encourage serious concentration, we'd decided to meet at Lauren's house rather than at the mall.

That was the good news. The bad news was that I couldn't be in two places at once. If I didn't show up for the meeting, my friends were going to be very unhappy campers.

On the other hand, how could I let Liam down? There were five of us on the committee. I was Liam's only backup. I felt like a juggler with too many balls in the air. How long could I keep this up before it all came crashing down?

You can do this, Mary-Kate, I thought.

"Okay, I'll be there," I promised.

Somehow I would find a way to make everything turn out all right.

chapter seven

"**Y**ou're kidding," Melanie said late that afternoon. We were gathered around the kitchen table at Lauren's house for the next meeting of the Spring Fling theme committee.

"Do I look like I'm laughing?" I countered. "I'm telling you, Aaron flunked guideline number one before school, and guideline number two at lunch. So far the score is Operation Aaron, two, Actual Aaron, nothing."

"Gee," Lauren said, sounding concerned as she reached for one of the snacks her mom had provided. "Maybe it wasn't such a good idea to test him on two guidelines in the same day."

"I didn't mean to!" I wailed. "It just sort of happened spontaneously."

"That could be important, you know," Brittany

put in. She took a sip of mineral water. "You weren't expecting the situation either, so your behavior couldn't influence what happened in any way. What's number two, again? Remind me."

I dug the guidelines out of my shoulder bag.

"'Guideline number two,'" I read aloud. "'How does he treat you when his friends are around? Is it: a) the same great way he treats you when you're alone? b) like some new toy he'd like to show off? c) like an embarrassing object to be ignored? If the answer's anything other than a), give him an *F* and move on.'"

"Good advice, I have to admit." Lauren nodded.

"That's pretty much what I thought," I said. "And for the record, ending up in category *c* is not much fun."

"He wouldn't even talk to you?" Melanie asked.

"Forget talking," I said. "He barely even looked at me." I scooped up a big glop of dip with a baby carrot, then chewed glumly. "I just don't get what's going on," I went on after a moment. "When Aaron called and said he wanted to talk about something important, the only thing I could think of was that maybe he wanted us to get back together. But if that's true, how come he keeps failing the guy-girl guidelines?"

"I still think you're focusing too much on what Aaron wants," Brittany said. "What about what *you* want, Ashley?"

"That's what I'm trying to figure out!" I cried. "That's why I'm using the guidelines."

"Okay, I get that," Brittany said patiently. "My point is that these guidelines are keeping you focused on Aaron. But what if he wasn't in the picture? How would you feel about going out with someone else?"

"I honestly don't know," I answered after a moment. "And before you ask, yes, of course I think math-class Michael is cute. But I'm not so sure it's a good idea to think about going out with anybody else right now. I'm really feeling like I've been burned, you guys. First Aaron, then that whole weird thing with Evan."

"If that's the way you feel, you probably shouldn't be seeing anyone else," Lauren acknowledged.

"At least not until I get this Aaron situation sorted out," I agreed. "I don't want to be in two relationships at the same time."

"Hey, there's this guy you ought to meet," Melanie said. "His name is Anthony Martin!"

"How are you doing with that?" I asked with a

quick pang of guilt. I'd been so busy focusing on my own situation, I'd all but forgotten about Melanie's recent painful encounter with two-timing Tony.

She gave a quick laugh. "Fine, really. I admit I did give myself one evening to be totally bummed. Then I decided, what was the point? The guy's obviously not serious about me, so why bother?"

"Speaking of 'serious,'" Lauren said. "When it comes to Spring Fling, we are 'seriously' behind. I know what we're talking about's really impor-tant . . ."

"But this is supposed to be a meeting," I fin-ished up. "I didn't mean to sidetrack us. Okay, let's get going."

"Aren't we going to wait for Mary-Kate?" Melanie asked.

Lauren shook her head, her expression tight. "We can't afford to. I don't know about you guys, but I'm really starting to feel the pressure. If we don't come up with a theme we can hand off to the decorations committee soon . . ."

Uh-oh, I thought. Lauren really *was* feeling the pressure, and Mary-Kate's lateness wasn't helping.

"Okay," I said, keeping my tone as upbeat as I could. "Let's hear what everybody has."

But inside I was worried. Missing this meeting definitely wasn't like Mary-Kate.

Where is *she?* I wondered.

❀

"I hope you don't mind carrying this one, too," Liam's second date said as she thrust a bag into his arms.

From where I was standing, I was pretty sure that brought the overall count to an even half-dozen, though the bigger bags *could* contain smaller ones that I couldn't see. That was a shopping technique I'd been known to use myself.

Liam's second date had been in full swing for about half an hour and showed no signs of slowing down. In fact, given the rate at which his date was making purchases, it might not end until she'd bought out the entire mall, in spite of the fact that each date was supposed to last no more than an hour.

The second date's name was Angela. She looked like a pixie, petite with curly red hair and a smattering of freckles across her nose. For ease of locating each other, she and Liam had met outside one of the coffee shops. Then they'd just sort of strolled the mall. I'd trailed along behind, doing my best imitation of a private eye. At first I'd been a little worried that Angela might catch on. She never even noticed me, though. She was too busy dragging Liam into almost every store they passed.

"I can't believe you suggested we meet at the mall," she gushed now. "It's just too perfect. The mall's my favorite place." She gave a giggle as she surveyed the bags. "Can you tell?"

"Absolutely," Liam answered. One of the bags he was carrying began to slip down his arm. He made a lunge to catch it, causing a chain reaction. It was as if he'd suddenly been sucked into some weird gravity vortex. One by one the bags dove for the floor.

"Oh, no!" Angela cried as she bent to help him scoop them up. Her voice came out squeaky. Her face was rapidly turning the color of her hair. "I never should have asked you to carry those, Liam. I'm so sorry."

"It's okay," Liam said, gathering up the fallen bags. "Don't worry about it."

"I probably shouldn't have bought all this stuff in the first place," Angela went on. "But I just . . ." She stopped, wringing her hands in a helpless gesture.

I felt a spurt of sympathy. All of a sudden I got

it. The poor girl was so nervous her behavior had turned out totally extreme. And now she was embarrassed, as well.

Well, of course she is, I realized. *On both counts.*

You always want to make a good impression on a first date. That goes without saying. Even under normal circumstances this can be hard. But Angela had the added pressure of having only sixty minutes. Add to that the fact that she didn't know Liam at all . . . It was sort of like speed blind dating. Going out with somebody you didn't know was always awkward. It was so hard to find the right balance.

That's it! I suddenly thought.

I snuck a quick glance at my watch. Date #2 would be over in about another ten minutes. If I could get my ideas down on paper quickly enough, I might still be able to make the Spring Fling committee meeting.

Moving past Liam and Angela so Liam would be sure to see me, I headed for the tables at the food court.

"Well, that was intense," Liam remarked several minutes later. He took a long swallow from the bottle of water he'd purchased, drinking as if he'd just run a marathon.

"Don't take this the wrong way," he went on when he could speak. "But I totally do not understand what just happened. What was all that shopping about?"

"I think I get it," I said. "That poor girl was completely freaked out. Shopping was a distraction, to help take her mind off how terrified she was."

"She must have been really scared," Liam said glumly. "My arms are actually sore." All of a sudden he sat up a little straighter. "Wait a minute. You're saying she was terrified of *me*? Thanks a lot!"

"Not you. The situation," I corrected him with a smile. "What you're really doing is going on a series of blind dates, Liam. I don't know why I didn't think of that before now. But watching Angela really made me see it. She just couldn't relax. It was tough for her, but I definitely got some great stuff for the next *Expertise* column."

"Let's hear it," Liam said.

"'How to Get Past the First Date, Pointer Number Two,'" I read, consulting my notes. "'When in doubt, chill out!'"

Liam chuckled.

"'A certain amount of nervousness on a first

date is perfectly normal,'" I went on. "'But sooner or later you have got to get your act together and settle down. The unexpected can be exciting, no two ways about it. But you can't get real if you can't find your comfort zone.'"

"Okay, that does it," Liam said suddenly. "I hate to do this, but I don't have a choice."

"Hate to do what?" I asked, startled. What had happened? I thought my pointer was right on the money.

"I'm going to have to ask for a meeting with CK and tell her she shouldn't have let you leave for another job. You are absolutely brilliant, Mary-Kate."

Happiness flooded through me. "Flattery will get you everywhere," I said with a smile. "But, honestly, I think you have the hard part. You actually have to go on these dates. All I have to do is watch and write down my conclusions. But so far I think you're striking out."

"Thanks a lot!" Liam cried in mock dismay. "What happened to moral support?"

"I am giving you moral support. I'm telling you the truth," I replied. "That's what friends do. Don't worry," I went on as his face stayed glum. "You just haven't met the right girl yet."

"Let's hope she shows up soon," Liam said.

She's already here, I thought. I was really falling for Liam. Hard. Thank goodness he only had one more blind date to go. Then I could get to work on my own project: convincing Liam that he and I would be the perfect couple.

❀

"Great day for a walk, huh?" said a voice beside me.

I jumped about a mile. Wrapped up in my own thoughts as I walked home from the recent and altogether useless Spring Fling committee meeting, I'd completely failed to notice anything or anyone around me.

"Oh, man, I'm really sorry," the voice went on.

I looked up. *Well, naturally,* I thought.

Math-class Michael was standing right next to me.

Okay, Ashley, I thought. *What do you do now?*

The truth was, Brittany was right. Michael Hennessey was definitely hot. He had a tall, trim build, dark brown hair, and eyes almost as green as Lauren's. A girl would have to be an idiot not to find him attractive.

But now is not a good time for me for me to start seeing anyone, I thought. *Not until I sort out the*

Aaron situation. Michael hasn't even asked you out, Ashley.

"Michael," I said, hoping my voice didn't sound quite as strained to him as it did to me. "Hi. Sorry, I was sort of zoned out. Lost in thought."

"My fault," he said quickly. "I sort of mentioned the weather. That's gotta be enough to scare anyone."

I smiled. Michael smiled back. A silence fell. Together we continued to the corner, then paused, watching the traffic.

"There's an opening," he suddenly said, reaching for my arm. "Come on. Let's go."

Before I knew what was happening, we were dashing across the street. I could feel my heart start to pump, and the firm grip of Michael's hand on my arm. As soon as we were on the other side, Michael dropped my arm, as if he suddenly realized he'd been holding on to me. A dull redness slowly spread across his cheekbones. I half expected him to make some excuse and walk away. But he stayed beside me.

"Going someplace special?" he asked.

"No," I answered. "Just home."

He was silent for another moment, as if considering something important.

"Okay if I walk you there?"

He really is *cute*, I thought. So many guys try to come across all smooth. It was sort of nice to be with one who got a little tongue-tied.

"Sure," I said. "Though I do know the way."

He gave a quick laugh, not minding that the joke was on him, and I found myself smiling in response. He would be easy to fall for. That was for certain.

Don't get carried away, Ashley, I scolded myself again. *Remember what you promised yourself.*

"So," he said after a moment. "You hang out with anyone much?"

"Well, there's Brittany Bowen. She's my best friend," I said, deliberately misunderstanding what he was asking. "And then there's my sister, Mary-Kate, of course."

"Okay," Michael answered, nodding quickly. "Yeah. Okay. Sure." We negotiated a second crosswalk. "But no, um, guys?"

"I'm not seeing anybody, if that's what you mean," I said. *Just say it, Ashley.* "In fact, for the moment, anyway, I've sort of sworn off guys. There's this thing I'm trying to work out, and until I do . . ."

"Okay, I get it," Michael said quickly.

"No," I said, surprising myself. I stopped walking. "I'm not sure you do. I'm not brushing you off, Michael. I'm telling you the truth. I think you're really nice . . ." I let my voice trail off. "But I just can't see anyone right now."

"Nice," he said.

"What?" I asked.

"You think I'm nice."

"Well, yes," I said, starting to feel a little flustered. "I do."

"That's it. I'm doomed. You know what they say about nice guys."

I felt a bubble of laughter swell inside my chest. He really *was* funny. He was cute, with a great sense of humor, and he was easy to talk to. And I was telling him to go away. Maybe I should have my head examined.

"Personally, I've never understood what's so bad about coming in last," I remarked as I began to walk once more. "The way I figure it, you win."

"How do you figure that?" he asked as he kept pace beside me.

"It means that nobody else comes after you."

He laughed. "I think you have a point," he said. "I just have one question."

"What's that?"

"How do you feel about guys who are nice *and* patient?"

I smiled again. I simply couldn't help it. "You'll be the very first to know."

It wasn't until a couple of hours later that I realized what had really happened. Michael Hennessey had done more than walk me home. He'd passed guideline #3 (*If he doesn't listen to you, listen to this: drop the guy, and find one who gets the message loud and clear.*) without even trying.

Which made the score: Michael, one, Aaron, nothing.

chapter eight

Two dates down, one to go, I thought.

And the truth was, I could hardly wait. Watching the guy I wanted to date going out with other girls, even for research rather than romantic purposes, was not precisely my idea of a great time. Only the fact that I'd never go back on a promise to help—and the fact that I wanted to keep an eye on things—had kept me from heading home.

Liam's third date was an informal dinner at this great new place called The Big Scoop. It was a replica of a 1950s soda fountain. All the wait-staff wore white pants, shirts, and paper hats. The floor was tiled with big squares of black and white linoleum. The tables were red, as were the vinyl seats. Each booth or table had its own mini-jukebox. Not only was the atmosphere fun, the ice cream, made on the premises, was to die for.

I'd arrived ahead of Liam and his final date, a girl named Sandra. I settled in at a table that would give me a good view of the entire restaurant. Seating was first come–first served, and you couldn't make reservations. I wasn't sure where Liam and Sandra would sit when they came in, but even if I wasn't close enough to hear their conversation, I had a good chance of being able to figure out whether or not the date was going well. You can tell a lot from body language.

I pictured Liam smiling, leaning forward, his eyes sparkling . . . and the girl across the table wasn't me. *Stop it, Mary-Kate,* I commanded myself. This wasn't a real date: it was research. Liam knew that as well as I did.

"May I take your order?"

"I'll have a hot fudge sundae," I said. "No whipped cream."

"Okay." The waiter nodded. "You want some extra hot fudge since you're skipping the whip?"

"Sounds good to me," I said. If I was going to indulge, I might as well go all the way.

"Gotcha."

He jotted down my order, stuck his pencil behind his ear, and walked off just as my cell phone started to warble. I pulled it out of my shoulder bag, and checked the caller ID. It was Lauren. Instantly I felt a wave of guilt roll over me. She probably wanted to know why I hadn't shown up for that afternoon's committee meeting, and there was no way I could explain. I'd promised Liam I wouldn't reveal my participation in *Expertise*. If I told Lauren the truth, I could get Liam fired.

On the other hand, she was my best friend, and I did owe her some kind of explanation. I punched the TALK button on the phone.

"Hi," I said. "What's up?"

"That's what I'm calling to ask *you*," Lauren said evenly. "We were supposed to meet this afternoon, in case you forgot."

Uh-oh. She's really mad, I thought.

"I didn't forget, Lauren," I said. "I just had . . . something come up. Something important. I can't really explain right now, but I will as soon as I can. I promise."

"Mary-Kate . . ." Lauren was close to losing it. I could tell by the sound of her voice.

"Look, Lauren," I said quickly. "I know it must look like I'm deliberately letting you down, but I don't mean to, honestly."

"I'm your best friend," Lauren said. "If this 'something' is so 'important,' how come I don't know about it?"

"Nobody knows about it," I said. "Not even Ashley. Believe it or not, I've actually been sworn to secrecy."

"What did you do? Join the CIA?"

"Darn. You figured it out. My cover's blown now and I'll have to retire."

There was a moment's silence. Then I was rewarded by a slight chuckle. "Good," Lauren said. "Then you can start showing up for meetings on time. You absolutely have to be there next time. We're still getting nowhere and we're all starting to panic."

"I'll be there," I promised.

At that moment the door of the Big Scoop opened. A girl with wavy dark hair and big brown eyes came in. She was wearing a sundress I'd ogled just last week at the mall. Liam was right behind her.

Showtime.

"Listen, Lauren," I said. "I've got to go. I'll see you at school tomorrow, okay?"

"Mary-Kate . . ." Lauren began.

Somewhat ruthlessly I ended the call and

turned off the phone. I couldn't afford any distractions. And I definitely couldn't afford to relax until Liam's third and final date was over.

This is a nightmare, I thought.

Even from all the way across the restaurant, I could tell that Date #3 was going well. Liam and Sandra hadn't stopped talking since they walked in the door. In fact, Liam was doing a pretty good job of enacting the nightmare fantasy I'd had before he arrived. He was leaning across the table toward Sandra, totally engrossed in what she was saying. When Liam sat back suddenly and laughed, I realized she must have told him a story or maybe a joke.

How to Get Past the First Date, Pointer #3, I wrote down in my notebook. *Make 'em laugh.*

At precisely that moment Liam laughed again, with Sandra joining in. They were really hitting it off. There was no way to deny it. *This was not supposed to happen,* I thought.

All of a sudden I didn't feel so well, and I didn't think it was because of the hot fudge sundae.

At least the date was almost over. According to my watch, which I'd been checking every twenty seconds for the last ten minutes, Liam and

Sandra's sixty minutes were almost up.

Once it's over, things will get back to normal, I thought. I told myself to stay focused on the positive. I'd never get Liam to see we belonged together if I had a bad attitude.

As I watched, Liam signaled for the waiter and paid the check. Then he and Sandra got up from the table and moved toward the door. They walked right by my table. Liam didn't even glance down. He opened the door, then followed Sandra out onto the sidewalk, the bell above the door pealing as the door swung closed behind them.

"Will there be anything else?"

My head jerked up. My waiter was hovering right above me. That was the moment I realized I'd been idly jabbing my spoon into what was left of my hot fudge sundae. Not that there was all that much, as I'd devoured most of it in my misery.

"No, thanks," I said. "I've had enough."

He whisked the dish away just as Liam came back through the door. He headed straight for my table.

"I can't believe it!" he exclaimed as he pulled out the chair across from me and plunked himself down. "I finally got it right! What's that saying? You know the one I mean."

I forced a smile. "Do you mean 'the third time's the charm'?"

"That's it. That's it exactly," Liam said. He shook his head, as if he still couldn't quite believe it. "That was really fun. You were right, Mary-Kate. All it took was the right girl."

But the right girl is supposed to be me! my heart cried. It was so simple. Why couldn't he see what was right in front of him the way I could?

"What did it look like from over here?" Liam asked.

"Just like what you're saying," I said, working to keep my voice even. "Like it went well. I even came up with a pointer: Make 'em laugh."

Liam smiled, remembering. "I guess I did laugh a lot, didn't I? I couldn't help it. She kept telling these funny stories about previous date disasters. I gotta tell you, it really broke the ice."

I'll bet it did, I thought. "How did she take it when you explained this was a one-date deal?" I asked.

Liam's faced went blank. "What?"

"These dates were supposed to be research for the column," I reminded him. "But you and Sandra really seemed to hit it off. I'm just wondering how she took it when you explained you

83

wouldn't be seeing each other again."

"We are seeing each other again," Liam said. "We're meeting at Click for coffee tomorrow morning."

A strange roaring sound filled my head. Maybe I hadn't heard him right. "What?"

"Sandra and I are meeting at Click Café for coffee before school tomorrow morning," Liam repeated happily, oblivious to my inner turmoil. "You're right about today's dates being research, but there's no reason I can't ask a girl out now that the research phase is over."

"You're going out with Sandra tomorrow morning."

Something about my tone must have finally gotten through. Liam's expression sobered. He leaned forward, staring across the table at me in obvious concern.

"Mary-Kate, are you all right? You keep repeating everything I say."

"I'm fine," I said. "Look, Liam, I've got to go. I'm behind on all sorts of stuff. I'll write up my ideas for the column, then e-mail them to you, alright?"

I shot up out of the chair and reached blindly for my shoulder bag.

"Wait, Mary-Kate," Liam said. He scrambled up after me as I headed for the door. "Look," he said, as he caught up to me on the sidewalk. "I got so carried away with working on the column that I didn't stop to think about how much time I've asked you to commit. If I've made things tough for you, I'm sorry."

I stopped. *This is why I'm falling so hard for him,* I thought. Liam was a genuinely nice guy. As far as I'm concerned, anyone who thinks nice guys finish last has never really met one.

"It's okay," I said, turning back. "Honestly, it is. I just need to get home." *Now. Before I lose it altogether.*

My input for *How to Get Past the First Date* had given Liam the tools he needed to do just that. With someone else.

Which left me with one very important question to ask—and answer—for myself: What on Earth was I going to do about it?

chapter nine

 N ew *day, new opportunities,* I told myself the next morning. *It's time for action, Mary-Kate.*

Now, if only I could decide what kind.

After a restless night spent trying to figure out what to do about the Liam-Sandra situation, I'd come to the following conclusion: I definitely could not afford to take it lying down. If I gave Liam up without a fight, I'd never forgive myself.

It wasn't that I didn't want him to be happy. It was that I didn't want him to be happy with somebody else. At about four A.M. I decided that keeping myself in the game should be my first priority. I couldn't afford to let myself get too far out of Liam's sight. If I did, I just might end up out of mind.

Ordinarily I'd have run my thoughts by Ashley.

But, as had been happening a lot lately, we'd also missed each other at night. When I got home from The Big Scoop, I found a note on the kitchen table saying that my dad had left on a sudden business trip, and Ashley had gone out to dinner with my mom. By the time they got home, I was already in bed. After the hot fudge sundae and the shock of Liam's decision to ask Sandra out on a second date, I'd needed an early night.

Not that I got any sleep.

Now I was having an early morning. Our school was a lot closer to Click Café than Liam's was, which meant he'd have to get there early. If I wanted to put in an appearance while he was there with Sandra, I was going to have to set a new personal record for getting out of bed and out the door.

It was one of those great spring mornings when you can smell the salt of the ocean in the air. The traffic was light between home and Click Café. And I was in luck. I found a space in the parking lot. I pulled in, then grabbed my bag and headed for the door before I could lose my nerve. I opened the door, rehearsing the excuse for being there I'd come up with the night before.

Liam wasn't there. But Aaron was.

He was sitting at a table near the window. There was a girl with him, one I wasn't sure I recognized. *Is that Suzanne, the new girl?* I thought. Our class had accepted a couple of transfers recently and I was still playing catch-up with the new names. Whoever she was, she seemed upset. As I watched, Aaron reached across the table to take one of her hands in his.

That's it! I thought. The thing Aaron wanted to talk to Ashley about. Not getting back together, but a new girlfriend.

Involuntarily I started forward. Behind me the door crashed shut. The girl's head jerked in my direction. I saw her eyes widen. Noticing the expression on her face, Aaron turned around. He and I made eye contact. I broke it first, moving quickly to get into the ordering line. Out of the corner of my eye, I saw him turn back around to the girl, talking rapidly.

No way Ashley knows about this, I thought. True, we hadn't seen much of each other the last couple of days, but I think she would have found the time to share information as important as this! *Who else knows?* I wondered. It couldn't be common knowledge at school yet. Both Ashley and I would have heard the rumors if it was.

Things like that are impossible to keep quiet.

I have to tell her. How am I going to tell her? I wondered. The line scooted forward. I ordered my drink, paid, then went to stand in the pickup line. I was so focused on Ashley's situation, I'd entirely forgotten about my own.

"Double tall mocha, no whip," the counter girl called out. I picked up my drink, then turned around. Maybe I moved too quickly. Maybe the drink was hotter than I expected. But the next thing I knew, my coffee was slipping from my fingers. As if it was moving in slow motion, I watched it fall. It hit the floor, exploding upward in a geyser of hot chocolate–y coffee, all over the pant legs of a guy standing behind me.

"Thanks a lot, Mary-Kate," a voice I recognized said.

"Liam," I croaked.

Before we could say any more, the staff at Click shot into action. "That's all right," my friend Malcolm said as he came out from behind the counter. He sopped up the spill with a dishtowel, then signaled another staff member to go for a mop and bucket.

"Don't worry. I'll get this cleaned up. Are you okay?" he asked Liam.

"Sure," Liam answered. "Fine."

"You already paid for your drinks, right?" Malcolm went on. "I'll get you a couple of vouchers for next time. What was your drink, Mary-Kate? Let me make you another one."

"I don't know what happened, Malcolm," I said. "I'm sorry I made such a huge mess. Don't bother getting me another drink."

"Of course I'm going to bother," Malcolm answered with a grin as he bent to retrieve the sopping wet cloth. "That's why they pay me the not-so-big bucks. Just hang for a second, okay?"

He headed behind the counter to wash his hands and get back to work. Liam and I stepped aside as the mop and bucket arrived.

"What is up with you, Mary-Kate?" Liam asked in a low voice. "I kept trying to get your attention in the drink line, but it was as if you were on another planet."

"I was . . . thinking about something," I said lamely. Over Liam's shoulder I was pretty sure I could see Sandra watching.

"You know you're not supposed to be taking notes anymore, right?" Liam asked. He leaned in close, making sure nobody else could overhear.

"Of course I know that," I hissed.

Liam straightened up. "Good," he said in a more normal tone of voice. "Because I'd hate to think—"

"You'd hate to think what?" I cut him off. "That I was following you on purpose? Get a grip. I come here all the time. It's my favorite coffee bar."

"I know that," Liam protested. "I just thought . . ."

"You don't have to explain," I cut him off again. "It's really pretty obvious. One successful date has done wonders for your ego."

Whoa, Mary-Kate, I thought. *Don't go too far. Calm down.*

Liam flushed. "Look," he said. "I . . ."

"Liam?" a new voice said.

Liam's head jerked around as if pulled by a string. "Sandra," he said. "Sorry. Hi."

"Is everything okay?" she asked. Her words were meant for him, but she was looking straight at me.

"Sure," Liam said. "Everything's fine. I just had a small but explosive encounter with Mary-Kate's beverage of choice."

"Oh," Sandra said. "So you guys know each other?"

"I'm Mary-Kate Olsen," I said, extending a

hand to shake hers before Liam could get a word in edgewise.

"Sandra Johnson," Sandra said. We shook hands as Liam stood by, looking helpless. "So," Sandra went on, "how do you know each other?"

"We . . . um . . ." Liam jumped in, trying to think of something on the spot. I could see Sandra's eyes darting between his face and mine as she drew her own conclusions.

Perfect, I thought.

Judging from Sandra's reaction, she was busy mistaking us for a former couple. Liam's unwillingness to explain how we knew each other had pretty much just clinched that.

"We used to—" Liam continued.

"Drink's up, Mary-Kate," Malcolm suddenly called out. "And here are those vouchers."

"It was great to meet you," I said to Sandra. "But I should get my drink and head out. I'm sorry about your pants, Liam."

"That's okay," he said.

I could feel two sets of eyes on me as I walked to the door. On sudden impulse I turned around to wave, my own gaze sweeping the coffee bar. That's when I realized that Aaron and his new girlfriend were gone.

My own situation was pushed to the back burner. *I have to get to Ashley!* I thought.

❋

Are you two speaking the same language when it comes to the language of love? If you don't mean the same thing by relationship, chances are good you haven't got one, at least not the one you want.

I closed my notebook, tucked it safely into my book bag, and squared my shoulders. *Okay, Ashley, you can do this,* I thought. More than that, I had to. Between Aaron's score on the first two guidelines and my conversation yesterday with Michael, I was feeling more confused than ever. Pretty much the opposite of what I'd hoped.

As far as I was concerned, this was a situation that could only be resolved in one way: I was going to have to do the very thing I'd been so actively avoiding. Talk to Aaron one-on-one. On my terms, though, not his. The way I had it figured, I could actually kill two guidelines with one conversation.

Guideline #3, which Michael had breezed right through yesterday without even trying, was all about whether or not a guy could listen. Guideline #4 was about getting a guy to talk. In the long run, though, both made similar points. Good communication was the key to a good relationship.

Alright, I thought, as I turned my steps in the direction of the library. *Let's get this show on the road.*

I decided I needed to talk to Aaron privately and in person, and did what my dad calls "taking the bull by the horns." I have no idea where parents come up with these phrases, but sometimes they do turn out to be appropriate. In this case it helped me realize that if I wanted to talk to Aaron now, I'd have to make the first move, especially since I'd been operating in avoidance mode until now.

I caught him right before school. His locker was only a few down from mine. When we'd been together, that was a good thing. After our breakup it had been kind of awkward, and we'd spontaneously developed the habit of using our lockers at different times. Today I altered my post breakup routine.

"Aaron," I said. "We have to talk."

He glanced up. I couldn't quite read the expression on his face. "My thoughts exactly."

I could feel the warmth start to creep up my neck. *Stay in control of the situation,* I scolded myself. "Meet me in the study carrels in the library during morning break," I said. Then, without another word, I turned and walked off.

My morning classes passed in a strange time warp. First period went way too fast. Second, way too slow. All during science lab, I saw Mary-Kate making weird faces, trying to get my attention. I shook my head. Not now. Much as I wanted to catch up on what was going on with her, I knew I couldn't afford to get distracted. I had to follow through on Operation Aaron.

Finally the bell rang for morning break and I headed to the library. By the time I got there, Aaron was already waiting for me in the study carrel we'd always used together. He was staring straight ahead, his expression serious. *We really did have a good time,* I suddenly thought.

I have no idea why seeing him so quiet and serious should have reminded me about how much fun he was. The truth is, before the misunderstandings set in, we'd been really great together.

"Hi," I said as I sat down.

Aaron looked up quickly. "Hi."

Yikes! I thought. This was even more awkward than I had feared it might be. *You want to know how well he communicates? Try doing it yourself.*

"I'm sorry I never called you back," I said, surprising myself.

"That's okay. I understand," Aaron said quickly.
"I suppose it must have been a surprise. I just—
Ashley, there's something we need to talk about."

I could feel my heart rate start to pick up.
"Okay," I said cautiously. "But first I have to ask
you something."

"What?"

"What do you think the word *relationship*
means?"

Aaron sat up a little straighter, looking startled.
"What?"

"Relationship," I said. "What do you think it
means?"

"Why do you want to know?"

"Any chance I could just get you to answer the
question?" I said.

I could see Aaron start to make a quick come-
back. But he caught himself short. He pulled in a
breath and answered slowly, as if thinking his
reply through as he spoke.

"A relationship is . . . a relationship," he said.
"Exclusive. Long-term. Serious. A thing that
makes me incapable of forming complete sen-
tences."

I couldn't help but smile. One of the things I'd always liked best about Aaron was his ability to lighten even the most serious situation.

"You mean like what we had?"

He was silent for a moment. "Yes," he finally answered, his eyes meeting mine. "Like what we had. Ashley, I never meant to hurt you. It just sort of . . . happened. We drifted apart."

"I know that, Aaron," I said.

Something flashed across his face. I thought it might be relief. *Here it comes,* I thought. He was finally going to tell me whatever it was he'd wanted to say.

At precisely that moment the bell signaling the end of morning break went off.

I shot from my seat as if bouncing up from a trampoline. "I have to go," I said. "I appreciate your being honest with me. It means a lot."

For a moment I thought he'd press the issue. But at the last second he seemed to change his mind. "It was good we could talk," he said. "I guess I'll see you around."

"Sure. See you around," I said. I headed for the door.

When I was about halfway to my next class, the truth suddenly dawned. Not only did we have the same definition of *relationship*, but *I* was the one who hadn't communicated very well. Aaron's score was really tied: two right answers to two wrong ones. When it came to today's guidelines, I was the one who'd flunked the course. Aaron had listened to me. I hadn't listened to him. Instead, I cut him off. The "something important" he'd wanted to discuss was still a mystery.

The only difference now was I wished I knew what it was about.

chapter ten

"Okay, so we're all agreed," Lauren said. "The theme for this year's Spring Fling is 'Woodland Wonderland.'"

Silence greeted her words. I glanced around the lunchroom table where the theme committee had finally managed to assemble. The truth is, none of us looked very enthusiastic.

"Don't everybody speak up at once," Melanie said.

"It has possibilities," Ashley admitted slowly. "Maybe we could do a *Lord of the Rings* elf/forest kind of thing. You know, kind of cool and sparkly."

"That would be good," Brittany seconded staunchly.

Lauren gave a quick glance in my direction, but it was Melanie who spoke up first. "What do you think, Mary-Kate?" she asked.

"I agree with Ashley," I said quickly. To be perfectly honest, I thought "Woodland Wonderland" had zero appeal, but I was hardly going to say that. "It does have possibilities."

"But you don't like it," Lauren said flatly.

"I didn't say that," I protested.

"You didn't have to, Mary-Kate," Lauren all but exploded. "You've hardly said a thing this entire meeting. When you do say something, you don't have anything positive to contribute. It's like you don't care at all."

"Of course I care," I said. "Look, you guys, I'm sorry I've missed meetings. But I'm here now. Can't we just concentrate on what needs to be done and forget about the past?"

"Arguing isn't going to get us anywhere," Ashley seconded.

"I know that," Lauren snapped. "I just think Mary-Kate could use a little attitude adjustment, that's all. First she doesn't show up, then, when she does show, all she does is diss our ideas. It's not like this was easy, you know."

"Okay, look," I said. "Give me twenty-four hours to redeem myself. If I can't come up with something we all like better by lunchtime tomorrow, we'll go with 'Woodland Wonderland.' I'll build the forest by myself if I have to."

"But that'll set us back another day," Lauren said.

"I think we should give Mary-Kate her chance," Brittany said. "It's the least we can do, as friends. I know your feelings are hurt, Lauren. Mine are, too. But that doesn't mean we shouldn't do the right thing."

"I agree with Brittany," Melanie said.

"I'm afraid it's unanimous," Ashley said. "I don't think waiting one more day is going to make things any worse as far as the dance is concerned, and if it can help us get our friendships back on track . . ."

"Okay, tomorrow at lunch," Lauren said. She stood. "I'll see you guys later." Then she walked away.

"Wow," Melanie said after a moment. "She's really mad."

"I guess I can't blame her," I said. "I know you all must feel I let you down. I had good reasons for what I did, reasons I can't explain now but will as soon as I can. I thought Lauren understood that."

"You can always talk to her later," Ashley said.

"After she's cooled down." Now she stood up, as well. "I've gotta jet. I have to go confess to Ms. Nelson that I'm withdrawing from the field hockey team."

"Field hockey!" Brittany said. "You hate field hockey."

"My point exactly," Ashley said.

Now's my chance to tell her about Aaron and the new girl, I thought. I started to rise.

"Ashley! Just the person I was looking for," a new voice cried. I watched as Janice, who sat behind Ashley in English, approached. "Any chance I can get your notes from yesterday's lecture on *The Merchant of Venice*?"

"Sure," Ashley said. Together the two moved off.

Oh, no! I thought. Every moment I delayed telling Ashley that I'd seen Aaron with another girl was another moment for her to find out in a way that might hurt or embarrassment her.

Tonight, for sure, I promised myself.

Thank goodness this day is over, I thought late that afternoon. I was completely down. I hadn't been able to talk to Ashley; my friends were angry with me. My relationship with Liam—the one I hoped for anyway—seemed just out of reach. Individually all my decisions over the last few days had seemed like good ones. So why couldn't I get them to add up?

Finally I'd decided to go for a walk along the beach, always my favorite place to clear my mind. I'd even turned down a ride from Ashley to do it. Now that school was out for the day, I didn't need to worry so much that she'd find out about Aaron and his new girlfriend on her own. I could tell her tonight.

It was my own head and heart I needed to work on in the meantime.

Maybe I'm going too fast, applying too much pressure to the situation, I thought as I walked along. Had it really been only a couple of days since Liam's first phone call? Since then I'd let working with him—thinking of him—completely rule my world. Maybe I needed to step back. Take a more Ashley-like approach.

I turned to start back down the beach and saw a couple coming toward me. They weren't holding hands, but they were engaged in animated conversation, her face tipped up to his. All of a sudden I felt my stomach clutch.

It was Liam and Sandra.

I can't let this happen! I thought. It didn't matter how much my brain was telling me to be patient; my heart was going to break if I let Liam get involved with another girl. I couldn't let him fall for someone else until he knew how I felt about him.

Though part of me wanted to run in the opposite direction, I quickened my pace. What's the one thing a new girlfriend, or even a girl hoping to be a new girlfriend, fears the most? The old girlfriend. And that's exactly what Sandra thought I was.

They say the best defense is a strong offense. I was going to fight for Liam—by sticking to him like glue.

"Hi, you guys!" My tone was cheerful and bright. Who cared if my behavior seemed phony and forced? In fact, that might be all for the good. Exactly the sort of behavior that would set off alarm bells in another girl's mind.

"Great to see you again," I said. "Twice in the same day. Wow. Go figure. Don't you just love the beach? I do."

They could probably see my back molars, my smile was so big.

Liam's eyes narrowed. His expression was both

confused and watchful. "Hi, Mary-Kate," he said. "What brings you here?"

I gave a trill of laughter. "You're kidding, right? I love the beach. You know that."

"Of course I do," he acknowledged. "What I meant was—"

"Why don't we all take a walk?" I interrupted cheerfully. "Since we're all here together. I mean, what could be better, right? That way Sandra and I can get to know each other and—"

"You know?" Sandra said suddenly. "I just don't think so."

I froze in my tracks.

Sandra turned toward Liam. "You're a great guy, Liam," she said. "And I think I could like you a lot. But not until you get your past sorted out. If that happens, I hope you'll call me. Until then . . ." She looked straight at me. "Don't bother."

"Sandra, wait. You don't understand," Liam said as she turned to go.

Sandra turned back, her dark gaze resting briefly on me. "I think I do," she answered quietly. "I might be getting some of the details wrong, but the big picture comes through loud and clear. Good-bye, Liam. It was nice almost getting to know you."

With that, she turned and walked off down the beach, leaving Liam and me alone.

He was silent for a moment, staring after Sandra. Then he turned to me. "I think you owe me an explanation, Mary-Kate," he said, his voice ominously quiet.

"I don't know what you mean—" I began.

"Look, just save it, okay?" Liam interrupted. "I thought you were my friend."

"I am," I protested. "You don't understand."

"What is there to understand?" he demanded. "I'm not sure what you thought you were doing, but if this is how you think friends treat one another, then I've got a newsflash for you. Maybe you're not the kind of friend I want to have."

With that, he turned and walked off.

Nice job, Mary-Kate, I thought. I'd just brought my own worst-case scenario crashing down on my head. Not only were Liam and I not together, but chances were good I'd lost his friendship, as well.

I'd wanted everything. But now it looked as if I'd end up with nothing at all.

chapter eleven

"**I**'m home!" I called out.

I paused, listening. The house was quiet. In the kitchen I discovered a note from my mom, saying Dad's business trip had wrapped up a day early and she'd gone to pick him up at the airport. I snagged a snack while I was there. There's nothing like seriously blowing things with a guy to kick a girl's sweet tooth into overdrive.

Heading down the hall to my room, I could hear Ashley's stereo. I thought I recognized Alanis Morissette, an artist Ashley only listens to when the situation is dire. *Uh-oh,* I thought. Had Ashley somehow found out about Aaron and his new girlfriend before I'd had the chance to tell her?

"Ash?" I said with a quick knock on the door.

Instantly the stereo went silent. Ashley opened

the door. Her expression was serious, but she didn't look as upset as I thought she'd be.

"May I come in?" I asked. "I was hoping we could talk."

"I was hoping so, too," Ashley admitted. She pushed the door all the way open. "I feel like I haven't seen you for days. It's seriously weird."

"Tell me about it."

We flopped down onto the bed, side by side. Lying on our backs, we stared up at the ceiling, where Ashley had recently mounted a few really cool posters of the night sky.

"Who goes first?" I asked, after a moment.

"I know!" Ashley suddenly exclaimed. She bounced up from the bed and moved to where her shoulder bag hung on the arm of her desk chair. Quickly she dug out her wallet and extracted a quarter. "Let's flip for it."

I felt my spirits lift a little. It was such a simple, silly thing to do.

"Heads or tails?" Ashley asked.

"Tails," I said.

She gave the coin a flick that sent it tumbling through the air. It landed beside me on the bed.

"Which is it?" Ashley asked.

"Heads," I said. "You win." I sat up, tucking my

feet under me, campfire style. Ashley sat down in her desk chair. "Do I get brownie points if I guess this has to do with Aaron?" I asked.

"Absolutely," Ashley said with a quick laugh. "But only small ones. It *is* pretty obvious. Okay, so, you remember I mentioned that Aaron called the other day and said he wanted to talk about something important?"

"Uh-huh." I nodded. *And I know what it is.* I'd wait to reveal what I knew, however. This was Ashley's turn to talk.

"And you remember I totally freaked?" she went on.

"I do seem to recall that," I said.

She took a deep breath. "Well . . ." she said. Quickly Ashley outlined her recent attempts to take control of the Aaron situation—specifically by using a series of guidelines she'd found on the *Girlz* Web site.

"Okay, wait a minute," I said, holding up a hand. "You mean the ones from *Expertise*, the new column?"

"Those are the ones," Ashley said. "I thought they made a lot of sense, and since they were written by a guy, I figured they'd work when it came to figuring out Aaron's behavior."

"I hate to tell you this," I said. "Actually, this is the thing I haven't been *able* to tell you, because I was sworn to secrecy. Those guidelines weren't actually written by a guy. I pretty much wrote them."

Ashley's mouth dropped open.

"You're kidding," she said. "Wait a minute. I remember. That phone call from Liam. Was it about the column?"

"He totally had writer's block, so he called to see if I could help." I shrugged. "I suggested some ideas, and CK liked them so much, she put them on the site a day ahead of time. If she ever found out Liam didn't write them alone, he could lose his job."

"She certainly won't hear it from me," Ashley promised at once. "But it does explain why I thought the guidelines were so right on!"

"Did they actually work?" I asked.

Ashley's expression grew thoughtful. "I'm still not sure," she confessed after a moment. "Right this moment the score is tied, two to two. Aaron totally bombed on the first two but passed the second two with flying colors. It's confusing, Mary-Kate."

"Ashley," I said, taking my own deep breath.

"There's something you should know. I saw Aaron holding hands with that new girl, Suzanne, at Click Café this morning."

"*What?*" Ashley cried.

"I stopped by Click Café this morning, for reasons I'll reveal in just a minute, and Aaron was there with Suzanne. They looked pretty close. I think that's what he's been trying to tell you. That he's found someone else."

Ashley was silent for a moment as she took this in. "That explains things," she said with a sigh. "All afternoon I've been tossing it around in my head, trying to figure out Aaron's weird guidelines score. You know the one about finding out if you have the same definition of the word *relationship*?"

"That was covered in number four." I nodded.

"Well, our definition is exactly the same," Ashley went on. "I couldn't figure out how that could happen if he didn't want to be with me. Now I know the answer. We do have the same definition of *relationship*. Aaron just doesn't want one with me anymore; he wants one with someone else."

"You don't seem very upset," I observed.

"You know something?" Ashley said thoughtfully. "I'm not. I'm relieved, if you want to know

111

the truth. When Aaron left me the voice mail saying he wanted to talk, I completely freaked out.

"I think it was because I knew in my heart I didn't want us to get back together. But I didn't know how I was going to tell him. I'd just gone through the pain of being rejected myself."

"I guess the guidelines worked after all," I said. "You just didn't have all the information you needed to interpret them."

"Hey," Ashley said, her expression brightening. "That's right! Now I can go talk to Aaron tomorrow knowing what I think he wants to tell me, and for sure knowing how I feel about it. Check it out: situation solved!"

"I wish I could solve mine so easily," I said.

"Okay, your turn," Ashley said at once. "Tell me what's wrong."

"It's Liam," I said. "I've totally fallen for him, but I've seriously blown it."

Now it was my turn to give a recap of my recent activities. When I explained about how I'd interfered with Liam's attempts to date Sandra and described Liam's reaction, Ashley winced.

"I hate to say this, but I'm surprised at you, Mary-Kate," she said. "Liam's right. You really didn't act like a friend."

Hard as this was to hear from the person who knows me best, I had to admit it was the truth.

"I know that," I said. "And I'm sorry. I truly am. And I know there's no excuse. The whole thing just seemed to happen so fast. But I do know I'm right about one thing. We could definitely be great together."

"What are you going to do now?" Ashley asked.

I was silent for a moment, thinking things over. "There's really only one choice," I said. "I have to apologize and hope for the best. If he can't accept my apology . . ." As the full impact of what this would mean hit home, my voice trailed off.

"That doesn't sound like Liam," Ashley said. "Once he's had a chance to cool down, I'm sure he'll understand."

"I hope so," I said. "What a weird week, huh? Both of us dealing with these guys from our past."

"No kidding!" Ashley laughed.

I think we both made the connection at the exact same moment. I saw her eyes widen as they connected with mine.

"Are you thinking what I'm thinking?" I asked.

"I hope so," she said.

Almost before she finished speaking, I dove for my cell phone, speed-dialing Lauren's number.

"Lauren, it's Mary-Kate," I said, rushing on before she could say anything or hang up on me. "Ash and I have just come up with what we think is the perfect theme for Spring Fling. How would you feel about . . . 'Blast from the Past'?"

Her response was instantaneous. "Perfect!" she exclaimed. "I love it."

"Why don't you call the others and come on over?" I suggested. "We can have a decorations brainstorming session. We can give some really good ideas to that committee, since I caused such a delay with ours."

"That's a great idea, Mary-Kate," Lauren said. There was a beat of silence. "I'm sorry I got so mad."

"Don't apologize. I understand," I said. "I'm just glad we're still friends."

"What are you talking about? Of course we are," Lauren said at once. "Keep saying stuff like that, and I'll *really* get mad!"

"One problem solved, one to go," I informed Ashley as I rang off.

Now, if only Liam would be as understanding.

chapter twelve

"So that's it," Aaron said. "Now you know. I'm dating Suzanne. I wanted to tell you before, only . . ."

"Only I went out of my way to make it impossible for you," I filled in. We were walking to school together, kind of like old times. As soon as the impromptu dance committee meeting had wrapped last night, I called Aaron and asked if we could meet the following morning.

He gave a slow smile. "It did feel that way," he admitted. He was silent for a moment, as if thinking something over. "You don't seem all that surprised," he finally said. "Mary-Kate said something, didn't she? I thought she might."

"Yes, she did," I said. "But, for the record, she didn't diss you at all. She just wanted me to know, so I wouldn't get caught by surprise at school."

"I was trying to avoid that, too," Aaron said with a nod. "We were friends before we started going out, Ashley. I'd really like it if we could be friends again. That's why I wanted to talk to you before I asked Suzanne to Spring Fling. I know our breakup hurt you. I'm sure there are things I could've handled better. I didn't want to hurt you any more."

"I appreciate that. I really do," I said. "And I hope you and Suzanne will be very happy together." Abruptly I stopped walking. "Stop me before I speak again," I said. "I sound like a sappy greeting card."

"I do have one question for you," Aaron said.

"Shoot."

"That meaning-of-the-word-*relationship* conversation. What was that about?"

"I was afraid you were going to ask that." I laughed. "It's kind of a long story." I filled him on Operation Aaron and my use of the *Expertise* guidelines.

"That is so weird," he said when I was finished. "I was taking a quiz and didn't even know it! How'd I do? On second thought, forget I asked."

"No way," I said. "You passed with flying colors.

Aaron smiled. "Friends?"

"Friends."

We reached campus and started across the lawn by the gym.

"And as your friend, I'd like to give you some advice," I went on.

"Uh-oh," Aaron joked.

I jabbed him in the ribs with an elbow. "Ask Suzanne to Spring Fling before the first-period bell rings," I said. "You've already wasted too much time."

Aaron stopped and looked into my eyes. "You really are the best, Ash," he said. "I'll see you around." Then he took off for the main school building at a dead run.

Final score: Operation Aaron, two, actual Aaron, three, I thought. We weren't getting back together, but somehow I felt that Aaron and I had both won anyhow. We'd been honest with each other and now we could be friends again.

Not only that, he'd just sailed right through guideline #5: *The guy you care about should make you smile.*

❀

"Thanks for agreeing to meet me, Liam," I said. I took a breath. "I know you probably didn't want to."

"I wouldn't say that," Liam answered quietly. "My guess is that we both want to clear the air."

"I like this place," I said as I took a look around. "It's nice."

Determined to put things right between us, I'd called Liam last night. I'd asked for a meeting but left the location up to him. He'd chosen a local park. It had turned out to be the perfect spot. It was hard to feel pessimistic while surrounded by happy kids climbing up monkey bars and flying through the air on swings. Though I knew the conversation would be difficult, my spirits began to rise as soon as I arrived.

I'd spotted Liam right away, sitting on a green park bench beside a small duck pond. My heart beating fast, I'd walked across the grass, then dropped down beside him.

"I suppose you're curious why I called you," I said, echoing his words at the beginning of our first meeting about *Expertise*. He got the reference at once.

"That was my line."

A small silence fell. "I brought my notes," I said. "That is, if you still want them."

"Of course I do," he said. He took them from me and stowed them in his backpack.

Come on, Mary-Kate, I thought. *Do the right thing.*

"I asked you to meet me because I want to apologize, Liam," I said. "You were absolutely right yesterday. I wasn't acting like a friend. I was acting like a jerk, and I'm sorry. I hope I haven't damaged our friendship beyond repair."

Liam was silent for a moment, staring at the ducks as they glided across the pond. My heart was beating so hard and fast, I feared it might explode right out of my chest.

"You couldn't do that, Mary-Kate," he finally answered. "I realized that after I calmed down. I didn't like what you did, and I'm still not sure I understand it, but I do know I want us to be friends."

A huge bubble of relief swelled inside me. I hadn't ruined everything after all. There might still be hope for us.

"I appreciate that," I said. *How on Earth am I going to explain?* I wondered. After all that had happened, how could I introduce the possibility of our becoming a couple?

"I was wondering," I said slowly as an idea began to dawn. "Do you suppose I could ask your advice about something?"

Liam turned to look at me in surprise. It was the first time he'd looked right at me since we started talking.

"Sure," he said. "What about?"

"I have this friend," I said, "who really likes this guy. But the situation's kind of complicated."

"In what way?" Liam asked. He switched his attention back to the duck pond.

"She and the guy are friends," I said. "She thinks she wants them to be something more. But she's not sure he sees the possibilities, and she doesn't know how to bring it up without risking the friendship."

"That's tough," Liam acknowledged. Again he fell silent for a moment. "Is the girl absolutely certain about her feelings for this guy?"

"Absolutely. Positively," I said, nodding vigorously. "There's not a doubt in her mind. In fact, she sort of got tunnel vision about it and recently engaged in some behavior she's pretty ashamed of."

"I see," Liam said quietly.

"So what do you think?" I asked, taking my courage firmly by the hand. "Do you think she can get him to change his mind about her? See her as more than just a friend?"

"Do you want me to answer honestly?"

"Of course I do," I said, praying I sounded more confident than I felt. Within the next few seconds I'd know whether or not Liam thought we had a future.

"No," Liam said. "I don't."

I could swear I felt my heart stop beating.

"She can't change his mind," Liam went on, "because that's a thing he has to do for himself."

"Okay, I can buy that. I see your point," I said as my heart began to function once more. "But is there anything the girl can do to, you know, sort of nudge him in the right direction?"

"I might be able to think of something," Liam said with a smile.

"Like what?"

"She might consider making the first move," Liam said. "Particularly if her behavior's been kind of off the charts. I think she owes it to both herself and the guy to do something that's easy to understand. That leaves no room for doubt. There's always the possibility that he's been confused, as well. He could be worrying that he's blown things."

"No way," I said at once. "He could never do that."

"Then tell him so. Better yet, show him."

"You think I should ask him out?"

"It's a possibility I think you should consider," Liam said. "And I thought we were talking about someone else."

"No, you didn't," I said, as I looked into his eyes.

"No," Liam said after a moment. "You're right. I didn't."

I could feel my heart beating hard and fast, but in an entirely different way than it had when the conversation started. This was the quick and heady beat of anticipation.

"So," I said, still holding his eyes. "There's this dance coming up. Any chance you'd like to go?"

"You'll have to do better than that, Mary-Kate," Liam said.

"I'd really like it if you'd go with me," I said. "Please say yes."

Liam smiled. "That wasn't so hard, was it?" he asked.

"What are you, nuts?" I cried.

He laughed then, and I could swear I felt my whole world click into focus. "Yes," he said. "To both questions."

chapter thirteen

"No two ways about it. You look fantastic!" Ashley said.

I took a quick turn in front of the mirror. In honor of the theme for Spring Fling, "Blast from the Past," I'd gone retro: I wore a fitted top, a full circle skirt that swished when I moved, and strappy sandals. It was a pretty fun look, I had to admit.

I turned to Ashley. "You don't look so bad yourself," I said.

After much urging from our friends, Ashley was attending the dance solo. Since she was going on her own, she'd decided on a look that was a little more traditional than mine: a formfitting dress in pale pink. Then she'd put her hair up, with a cascade of curls splashing down her neck.

The doorbell rang. "Omigosh! That must be Liam."

Ashley reached to give me a hug. "I'm really happy for you, Mary-Kate," she said. "And I'm proud of you, too. You took a big chance telling Liam the truth about how you felt."

"It was pretty scary," I admitted. "But worth it, too. I really think we're going to be great together, Ash."

"There's a young man in my living room claiming that a Mary-Kate Olsen lives here." My father's voice drifted down the hall. "If she doesn't put in an appearance in the next twenty seconds, I'll be forced to tell him he's come to the wrong address."

"Dad!" I wailed. I started down the hall.

"Works every time," I heard my father confide to Liam.

As I was moving toward the foyer, I could see Liam in his retro look: a black leather jacket, jeans, and white T-shirt.

And he was holding a corsage the exact color of my skirt.

❋

"May I have this dance?" a voice inquired. "Though, on second thought, we could sit down, too. These shoes are new, and they're killing me."

I turned and looked into Michael Hennessey's smiling green eyes. I'd seen him a couple of times since I'd arrived at the Spring Fling, dancing with a different girl each time. I was hoping this meant what I thought it did: that he'd come stag, as well.

"I didn't think guys admitted things like that," I said.

"Not insecure guys," Michael agreed. "I, however, am afraid of nothing." The smile faded as he continued to gaze into my eyes. "Except maybe the fact that you're here with someone else."

About a million possible responses flitted through my mind. I rejected all but one. It was time for a direct approach.

"I'm not," I said. "In fact, you know that conversation we had earlier—the one when I said I'd sworn off guys?"

"I remember," Michael said. The smile began to creep back into his eyes.

"I'm now officially over that," I said.

"Oh."

I'd sort of hoped for a bigger reaction, I admit. I stood on tiptoe, as if trying to see over Michael's shoulder.

"How come I don't see *your* date around?"

"That would be because I haven't got one,"

Michael answered. "Looks like we're both here on our own."

"Looks like it," I agreed. "So, do you want to dance or sit down?"

His face took on the intent expression it had the other day when we'd talked. It packed quite a punch.

"That depends."

"On what?"

"Who gets the last dance?"

Oh, man, I thought. It looked as if "Blast from the Past" was going to be the start of something special for both Mary-Kate *and* me.

"You do," I said.

"I was really hoping you'd say that."

I was smiling as I moved into his arms.

Find out what happens next in

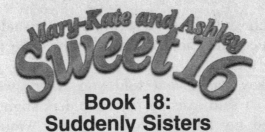

Book 18:
Suddenly Sisters

"I can't believe we're still talking about this," I said over my shoulder to my sister Ashley. "I've apologized about a million times."

We were standing in line at the cafeteria at school, waiting to pay for our lunches. For the fifth time that day, she had brought up the dress that I had borrowed for my date the weekend before. Well, borrowed and then ruined by spilling ketchup all over it.

"I just wish you had been more careful," Ashley replied, digging through her bag for her wallet. "I mean, that was my favorite dress."

She paid for our food and I led the way

through the cafeteria toward our usual table. Melanie Han and Brittany Bowen were already sitting there.

"Okay, say I *had* told you where we were going," I said, raising my shoulders slightly as I gripped my tray with both hands. "Would you have really said 'no'?"

Ashley paused and looked at me. I knew I had her. Neither one of us ever said 'no' when the other one wanted to borrow something.

"Okay, no. I wouldn't have said 'no,'" Ashley said finally, rolling her eyes. She flipped her long blonde hair over her shoulder as she sat down. "But you still should have been more careful."

"All right, all right," I said, dropping into the chair next to Melanie. "I swear it will never happen again."

"Thank you," Ashley replied with a smile. "See that's all you needed to say. And I promise I'll never take any of your stuff without thinking about where I'm going first."

"Deal," I said.

"I can't believe it," Melanie said with a gleam in her dark eyes. She put her book away and turned her attention to us. "You guys are *still* talking about the dress?"

"Not anymore, hopefully," I told her.

"Sheesh! At least it's only one dress, Ash," Brittany said. "I can't even tell you how many of my outfits have hit the dumpster since my brother Lucas was born."

"What do you mean?" Ashley asked.

"The kid's like a walking disaster," Brittany said. "I mean, when he's not spitting up on you, he's throwing his food or knocking stuff over. And don't even get me started on the diapers."

"Oh! But he's so cute!" I said, thinking of baby Lucas's pudgy little cheeks and his dimpled arms and legs.

"Oh please," Brittany said. "I love the little guy, but my life has been insane since he came along."

"Well, when there's a baby around, you have to expect that kind of thing," Ashley said with a shrug. "Mary-Kate ruining my stuff is more *un*expected."

"All right! That's it! I'm never touching your stuff again!" I said with a laugh. "It's been decided!"

"Please! You guys, at least you *have* someone to borrow stuff from. You should appreciate it," Melanie said. "It stinks being an only child."

Ashley and I exchanged a look. Melanie's father was a fashion designer—that was where she got her eye for costumes. She hardly ever wore the same outfit twice.

"Why would you need to borrow stuff?" I asked. "Your dad brings home an entire new wardrobe for you every season."

"Yeah, Mel. You have the life," Ashley added.

"And I don't care what you say, Brittany," I put in. "I would love to have a little baby brother."

As I dug into my lunch, I saw Brittany and Melanie exchanging a mischievous look.

"What?" Ashley asked them.

"I was just thinking," Brittany said, folding her arms on the table. "If you guys think our lives are so great, why don't you come stay with us for a little while and see for yourselves?"

"Yeah. Ashley can stay with me and see if I really have 'the life,'" Melanie said. "And Mary-Kate can go stay with Brittany and the adorable baby."

"For how long?" Ashley asked, her eyes lighting up. Clearly she liked the idea.

"I don't know," Brittany said. "A week?"

I looked at Ashley across the table and we both smiled slowly. This could be very interesting.

"Sounds like fun," I said finally.

"Yeah," Ashley added with a nod. "We're in."

Mary-Kate and Ashley Sweet 16
$500 Shopping Spree Sweepstakes

OFFICIAL RULES:

1. **No purchase or payment necessary to enter or win.**

2. **How to Enter.** To enter, complete the official entry form or hand print your name, address, age, and phone number along with the words *"Sweet 16* Win A Shopping Spree Sweepstakes" on a 3" x 5" card and mail to: *"Sweet 16* Win A Shopping Spree Sweepstakes" c/o HarperEntertainment, Attn: Children's Marketing Department, 10 East 53rd Street, New York, NY 10022. Entries must be received no later than June 28, 2005. Enter as often as you wish, but each entry must be mailed separately. One entry per envelope. Partially completed, illegible, or mechanically reproduced entries will not be accepted. Sponsor is not responsible for lost, late, mutilated, illegible, stolen, postage due, incomplete, or misdirected entries. All entries become the property of Dualstar Entertainment Group, LLC and will not be returned.

3. **Eligibility.** Sweepstakes open to all legal residents of the United States (excluding Colorado and Rhode Island), who are between the ages of five and fifteen on June 28, 2005 excluding employees and immediate family members of HarperCollins Publishers, Inc., ("HarperCollins"), Parachute Properties and Parachute Press, Inc., and their respective subsidiaries and affiliates, officers, directors, shareholders, employees, agents, attorneys, and other representatives and their immediate families (individually and collectively, "Parachute"), Dualstar Entertainment Group, LLC, and its subsidiaries and affiliates, officers, directors, shareholders, employees, agents, attorneys, and other representatives and their immediate families (individually and collectively, "Dualstar"), and their respective parent companies, affiliates, subsidiaries, advertising, promotion and fulfillment agencies, and the persons with whom each of the above are domiciled. All applicable federal, state and local laws and regulations apply. Offer void where prohibited or restricted by law.

4. **Odds of Winning.** Odds of winning depend on the total number of entries received. Approximately 300,000 sweepstakes announcements published. Prize will be awarded. Winner will be randomly drawn on or about July 15, 2005, by HarperCollins, whose decision is final. Potential winner will be notified by mail and will be required to sign and return an affidavit of eligibility and release of liability within 14 days of notification. Prize won by a minor will be awarded to parent or legal guardian who must sign and return all required legal documents. By acceptance of the prize, winner consents to the use of their name, photograph, likeness, and biographical information by HarperCollins, Parachute, Dualstar, and for publicity purposes without further compensation except where prohibited.

5. **Grand Prize.** One Grand Prize Winner will receive a $500 cash prize to be used at winner's discretion.

6. **Prize Limitations.** Prize will be awarded. Prize is non-transferable and cannot be sold or redeemed for cash. No cash substitute is available. Any federal, state, or local taxes are the responsibility of the winner. Sponsor may substitute prize of equal or greater value, if necessary, due to availability.

7. **Additional terms:** By participating, entrants agree a) to the official rules and decisions of the judges, which will be final in all respects; and to waive any claim to ambiguity of the official rules and b) to release, discharge, and hold harmless HarperCollins, Parachute, Dualstar, and their respective parent companies, affiliates, subsidiaries, employees and representatives and advertising, promotion and fulfillment agencies from and against any and all liability or damages associated with acceptance, use, or misuse of any prize received or participation in any Sweepstakes-related activity or participation in this Sweepstakes.

8. **Dispute Resolution.** Any dispute arising from this Sweepstakes will be determined according to the laws of the State of New York, without reference to its conflict of law principles, and the entrants consent to the personal jurisdiction of the State and Federal courts located in New York County and agree that such courts have exclusive jurisdiction over all such disputes.

9. **Winner Information.** To obtain the name of the winner, please send your request and a self-addressed stamped envelope (residents of Vermont may omit return postage) to *"Sweet 16* Win A Shopping Spree Sweepstakes" Winner, c/o HarperEntertainment, 10 East 53rd Street, New York, NY 10022 after August 15, 2005, but no later than February 15, 2006.

10. **Sweepstakes Sponsor:** HarperCollins Publishers.